Darkhenge

CATHERINE FISHER

Darkhenge

Greenwillow Books
An Imprint of HarperCollins *Publishers*

Darkhenge
Copyright © 2005 by Catherine Fisher
First published in 2005 in Great Britain by The Bodley Head, an imprint of
Random House Children's Books.
First published in 2006 in the United States by Greenwillow Books.

The right of Catherine Fisher to be identified as the author of this work
has been asserted by her.

The text of this book is set in Cochin. Book design by Sylvie Le Floc'h.

Library of Congress Cataloging-in-Publication Data
Fisher, Catherine
Darkhenge / by Catherine Fisher.
p. cm.
"Greenwillow Books."
Summary: Worried about his sister Chloe's comatose state after a riding accident,
teenage Rob, in an effort to distract himself, gets a job on a secretive local archeologi-
cal dig and finds himself drawn into a mysterious world of magic involving a powerful, centuries-old, shape-shifting Druid called Vetch who promises to help retrieve his
sister from the "unworld" of her coma.
ISBN-10: 0-06-078582-9 (trade bdg.) ISBN-13: 978-0-06-078582-6
ISBN-10: 0-06-078583-7 (lib. bdg.) ISBN-13: 978-0-06-078583-3
[1. Magic—Fiction. 2. Space and time—Fiction. 3. Druids and druidism—Fiction.
4. Brothers and sisters—Fiction. 5. Archaeology—Fiction. 6. England—Fiction.]
PZ7.F4995Dar 2005 [Fic]—dc22 2004054159

First American Edition 10 9 8 7 6 5 4 3 2 1

 Greenwillow Books

Darkhenge

The
Cauldron-Born

B. BEITHNE: BIRCH

"Eat," he keeps saying. "Eat," but I won't. If I do I may be
trapped here forever, and I'm not even hungry. He leaves me alone
if I scream at him; he doesn't like that.

Outside the door of the room are endless corridors. I've
explored them for miles. At least I think I have. They all look the
same—stone-flagged and cobwebbed. Empty. There are sounds in
the building. They echo distantly, but I don't know what they are.
Sometimes I come across a window, and scrub dirt off tiny leaded
panes to look out. It's hard to be sure, but the sky here seems a
sullen, dim twilight. It never gets darker or lighter, but there are
faint stars in strange constellations, billions of them.

What scares me most, though, are the trees.

There are trees everywhere. Tangly and green, pushing right
up against the walls, tapping and knocking.

As if they wanted to get in.

The oaks shimmer, the stream runs cold.
Happy is he who sees the one that he loves.

∞ THE BOOK OF TALIESIN

The tree branched like a brain.

It was the same as the diagram in his biology textbook, a tangle of neurons and dendrites and synapses. It was what was in him now, working his eyes and fingers. So ingenious. So fragile.

He bent over the page, noticing how his shadow was ultramarine blue on the white cartridge paper; with the side of the pencil he shaded in the edge of the bough, feeling the soft fibers of carbon darken the grain. He marked a few quick cracks, then cross-hatched the hole in the trunk, rubbed splotches of lichen, enjoying the skill in his hands, the way drawing it made him and the tree one creature.

A drop of rain spatted on the page.

Rob looked up. His concentration snapped like a thread.

Clouds were looming in from the north. They were black and heavy; already he could see the leading edge as a gray smudge drifted over the miles of open downland, masking the low hump of Windmill Hill and its barrows. "It's raining," he said.

From the high grass a tinselly whisper of music rose and fell.

"Dan! We're going to get soaked."

A hand played air guitar to inaudible riffs.

Rob glanced around. There were a few thorn bushes to shelter under, but not much else. The white chalk track of the Ridgeway ran away on each side along the exposed crest of the downs. Below in the fields, acres of barley waved.

He kicked the sprawling figure; Daniel sat up, annoyed. "What?"

He said it too loud, the earphones deafening him. Rob reached over and tweaked them off. "Come on. I'm hungry. We're going."

"Right in the middle of the best bit." Dan turned the CD off and rubbed his numbed ears. "So where's the masterpiece?"

"Show you later. Come on."

"Home?"

"No. Avebury."

These days he never wanted to go home. It was Tuesday and Maria would be there, and she irritated him, filling the gloomy rooms with her cheery Italian chatter. They couldn't do without her, but he didn't have to be there to put up with it. He slid the sketchbook into the backpack and snapped the pencil tin shut.

The bikes were tangled together in the long grass. Dan tugged his front wheel out. "Three more lessons, max. No more bikes then, Robbie boy."

Rob grinned. "Sure." Danny had already taken the driving test twice. If he failed again his mother had said she wouldn't pay for any more lessons, and if he did pass she wouldn't let him near her car. So either way he was an optimist.

Rain was spitting. "Green Street?" Rob asked.

"Too far. The track under the barrows. Down to the lane."

Then he was gone, riding fast, the earphones jammed back in, speeding off to heavy metal. Rob stared after him, stricken. Dan had forgotten. In the three months since the accident, they had never gone down that track.

Or maybe he hadn't forgotten; maybe it was deliberate. Rob had to face the place sometime, and it was best to do it now, without thinking too much. He climbed on the bike and cycled, head down.

There were poppies in the fields, like something from Monet, splashes of red. Those on the grass near the track were chalk-whitened, powdered from passing trail bikes and the heavy clump of hikers' boots. Now big raindrops spatted beside them into the dust. All across the fields the golden crop bowed and shivered, as the approaching storm shredded its peace.

The Ridgeway was rutted, its dry hollows and tire tracks

hardened into solid ledges; the bikes bumped and slewed through and over them. No one else was up here today; raising his head Rob could see the parking lot on Overton Hill was empty, and beyond it the trucks on the A4 roared down toward Silbury, their windshields glinting in the ominous light. All the wide downland seemed to cower under the gathering wind, and as the bikes turned into the barley and rattled down to the barrows, he breathed in the rapidly cooling air, its sweet mingled summer smells, the sourness of crusted horse dung, the spatter of insects.

Dan was well ahead. The track dropped beneath a trio of barrows, each darkly crowned with crowded copses of beech trees. As he rode under them, he saw the swell of the burial mounds, one side scraped raw where some kids had rigged a rope and dragged their feet in the white chalk. He was riding full into the wind now and the rain stung his face; he kept his head down, marveling how the weather on the downs could change so fast. Already the rain was pelting, each drop a hardness. The front of his T-shirt was soaked.

Dan was cycling recklessly. He hated getting wet and was careless about the rutted track, taking the bends with insolent speed. Rob was more careful. The backpack, jammed full of tins of pastels and a bulky sketch pad, bounced on his shoulders; he raced across the downs at a crazy angle, and there was no shelter from the horizontal storm until the overgrown hedgerow along the track down to Falkner's Circle.

The turn was too sharp. He skidded, chalk stinging out under his back wheel. The bike heeled over, hit a stone.

Suddenly he was off balance, knew that nightmarish moment of going too far ever to be upright again, got his foot down, but the bike's weight shot from under him, and he went sprawling.

"Bloody hell!"

He picked himself up, kicked the bike, and looked at his hands. Chalk lumps rolled from indentations in his skin. One palm was grazed, its black smear filled with tiny beads of blood.

Rob blew out his cheeks and looked down the track. Dan was probably already at the road by now. He crouched quickly, picking up the scatter of pastels that had burst from their box. They were the fat soft ones, expensive and crumbly, and hidden in the wet long grass. He snatched them and jammed them back: yellow ocher, burnt sienna, sage green, all the landscape colors he spent his allowance on most Saturdays in Marlborough. Many were in small pieces, their paper tubes half hollow. The Vandyke brown was missing; he hunted for it, and swore when he found it crushed under his heel.

A horse brushed past him.

He turned in alarm. It had come up the track incredibly silently, a white horse, and as it strode away, its rider ducked low under the overhanging straggle of birch and hawthorn. From the back the horse seemed huge, its tail swishing against flies. The rider wore red, a girl, her hair cropped and fair and straight. Like Chloe's.

He looked away instantly, flinching from the memory, scrabbled for the dusty fragments of Vandyke brown, thrust them in the box, tossed it in the backpack, and swung the whole thing on his back. Grabbing his bike, he hauled it up.

The horse was shimmering. Whether it was the hot afternoon or the glitter of the rain that was hammering down now, something was filling the air with light, a glinting, slashing brightness, and the horse was walking into it.

Rob stood still a moment. Then, wheeling the bike, he hurried after it.

It was too far ahead. The bike wheels jolted, but always the horse was just out of sight, behind bushes, round a slight bend. Anxious, nagged by an inexplicable fear, he shoved through the leaves after it, the black rubber handles of the bike sticky in his fingers. The afternoon hushed; noise ebbed away. His senses were suddenly acute, the smell of the grass pungent, a faint coconut aroma of gorse, sickly sweet. Every fragment of chalk his wheels crushed seemed crackingly loud.

In the shimmering heat he came to Falkner's Circle.

It hardly existed. One great stone, taller than him, lay toppled, pierced and used as a gatepost, and another sprawled half-buried in the undergrowth. But the space was palpable, the emptiness tingled on his skin; he could see it though there was nothing there to see, the space the stones had once surrounded. And the horse was walking into it.

Rob stopped, breathless. "Chloe?" he whispered.

The girl looked back. Her face was shadowed by great trees, their branches so low she had to duck under them. The sun shafted through forest.

He wasn't sure. Green flickers, motes of dust in golden light. Hooker's green, sage green, a million greens. A narrow face, a smile like hers, not seen for three months, except in photographs. An impudent, spiteful smile. And a voice. It said, "Hi, Robbie."

He was shivering.

He was icy with sweat, drenched with rain.

It couldn't be her.

There was no circle. He knew it, and as he knew it the birdsong came back, and the spatter and crash of rain; there was no forest here or anywhere for miles, and the horse had gone too far down the track for him even to see.

He pulled the bike upright, pushed off, and pedaled. In the shelter of the hedge he pelted down, ducking leaves, skirting ruts, skidding out into the emptiness of the paved road, just missing a car that blared its horn angrily and swerved.

Dan was propped against the wooden fence opposite; nervously he straightened. "Be careful!" As if he'd just remembered this was the place the accident had been.

"Where is she?" Rob gasped.

"Who?"

"The girl on the horse."

Dan looked at him in disbelief. Then he said, "What horse?"

There was no horse. It was quite obvious, and it terrified him. On each side the downs were wide open and empty, the rain raking the crop. The road ran visible for at least a mile. Even the tourists had scattered from the downpour.

He could see the whole world.

There was no horse.

Dan was looking at him unhappily. "You okay?" His

voice was subdued. "We shouldn't have come this way. I should have thought. Sorry."

Rob didn't know what to answer. So he got on his bike and pedaled toward Avebury, wobbling a little, then going fast so Dan wouldn't catch up.

There was no real way to think about it. The shock of the horse not being there was like an electric jolt inside him; it seemed to fracture the world, was a black crack down the screen of his mind. It had been real, had brushed his side with its flank, had crushed the grass, had clinked, been heavy.

And the girl had said his name.

But it wasn't Chloe. That would be an extra terror, because Chloe was in the nursing home, lying in the bed in the expensive room, with the tubes in her arm and the electronic monitors throbbing all around her. And his mother wiping the dribbles from her mouth.

Dan sped past him. "I'm an idiot, Rob," he muttered.

For once, Avebury was fairly quiet. Usually on summer afternoons the grass between the ancient stones was a patchwork of picnicking tourists or Reiki practitioners or groups beating drums around the obelisk marker. But the rain had driven them in, to the tea rooms or the museum, or maybe into Avebury Manor for the guided tours. Splashing up the main street through the constant stream of traffic that ran through the village, Rob watched Dan ride into the pub parking lot, dodge some travelers and their dogs, and disappear around the back.

He rode after him, more slowly.

Propping the bike in the shed full of chopped logs, he went in.

Midafternoon, the Red Lion was busy. Dan's mother worked here. She came over, took one look at Rob, and said, "Have you two had any dinner?"

"What, with Leonardo da Vinci drawing anything that moves?" Dan grabbed a packet of chips from a box. Efficiently, she took it from him.

"Then I'll get you something decent. Go into the dining room and find a table."

Dan's mother was short and patchily blond, an unnatural yellow that jarred on Rob every time he saw her. Now he focused his distaste on her blowsiness, the way she said *dinner* instead of *lunch*, her red fingernails. It helped. It made him feel better, even though he liked her. It blotted out the girl and the horse.

They had lasagne and fries and it was hot and tasty. Dan dolloped tomato ketchup on his.

"Peasant," Rob muttered.

"Afraid so. Not been to Italy, me. Not cultured."

"You can say that again."

Dracula-like, Dan leered through two fry-fangs. Rob made the effort and laughed, though they both knew he didn't want to. Neither of them said anything about Falkner's Circle.

The room was full, with a comforting, steamy heat. In the window seat Americans from a tour bus, their accents loud and strange, ate and argued over maps. At the next table were some archaeology students; Rob knew them by sight because they were staying at the B and B down the road from Dan's house. One of the girls was very pretty; Dan leaned across. "Get an eyeful of her."

"She'd make a great model."

Dan grinned. Then he said, "Ask her."

"Don't be stupid."

"I will then." Before Rob could move, he'd turned. "Hello. Excuse me. My friend is an artist. He wonders if you'd model for him."

They all stared at Rob. "Shut up, Dan," he muttered, furiously red.

The girl said, "How much do you pay?" She was straight faced, but the others were grinning.

One man picked up their bill and went off with it; another snorted and said, "She's too old for you, kid."

"Forget it," Rob muttered. "Honestly, it's just him. He's an idiot. He's always like this."

She smiled. "Well, I'm flattered. But sorry, I'm going on holiday tomorrow. Are you any good?"

She was just being nice. Dan seemed to think it was for him. "He's the best. Doing art at university next year."

"Which one?"

"I'm not sure. . . . I'm getting a portfolio together. . . ." Rob was mumbling stupidly. He didn't want to be talking to her about this, he didn't even know her, but they were going now, all her smirking friends, and she was standing up. Then she turned, and her smile had gone.

"Look. Seriously. They need someone out on the new dig to do drawings, recording finds. With the holidays everyone's away."

"What dig?" Dan asked.

She frowned. "It's a big secret. Something unusual. In a field over toward East Kennet. Ask for Dr. Kavanagh; you might be just what they need."

She picked up her jacket and then turned back. "Don't say I sent you, mind. No one's supposed to talk. Though they won't be able to keep it quiet for long."

"Keep what quiet?" Dan was overacting; his eyes were wide.

She smiled and shrugged. As if she was already regretting saying anything about it.

L. LUIS: ROWAN

I was on Callie and we were riding down to the lane.
Something came along. It wasn't a car. Or was it?

It was big and dark and we rode through it like a gateway,
and when I dismounted he was waiting on the other side, in the
courtyard of this house. "Welcome to Royal Castle, Chloe," he said.
On the banners behind him were three cranes, on a bull's back.

He always wears a mask, of rowan leaves with a few orange
berries. His eyes watch me carefully.

I think . . . Well, I think it's possible I may be dead.

I speak what no one else can speak.

∞ THE BOOK OF TALIESIN

They sprawled in the grass by the Outer Circle, near the Barber's Stone, which had once fallen and crushed a man in the fourteenth century. Lying on his back, Dan squirmed beneath its perilous overhang so that the shadow fell across his face.

"Don't," Rob muttered, uneasy.

"This thing must weigh tons. He'd never have felt a thing. Splat!"

Rob didn't answer. He sat away from the vast sarsen, cross-legged and uncomfortable. To him it never felt right even to lean against one of them; they were treacherous and dangerous things, always cold. The eternal puzzle of why they were there kept his mind from accepting them; the faces he imagined in their profiles were sinister, and their lichen-splotched leanings, their seamed and root-holed salmon and cream colors were too strange.

He tossed the pencil down and lay back. The sky was spattered with cloud, its gaps blue.

"You could find this dig," Dan said after a while.

"Why don't you?"

"I've already got a job." He looked over. "They might pay you."

"Don't need the money." It was boasting, but true.

Dan snorted, because during the holidays he spent most afternoons in the back room of the Lion washing glasses and wiping tables for a pittance.

"It'll keep you from thinking about things."

They were silent, Rob stricken again by the glimpse of the girl on the horse, and Dan worried too, probably, because he wriggled out from the vast stone and rolled over. Rob had a sudden premonition that Dan was working himself up to ask about Chloe, whether there was any change in her condition; they both knew it was a forbidden topic, so he said quickly, "God. Just look at this lot."

A colorful group was trooping through the wooden gate, probably from the tents and benders that were always pitched in the tree clumps at the foot of Green Street. There were about a dozen of them, men and women with a few young kids, dressed in the usual dippy mix of camouflage gear and washed-out tie-dye. They came and stood in a circle around the next stone but one, choosing the spot carefully, circling it, tossing out handfuls of herbs. Then they joined hands and sang. Dan snorted in scorn. But then, this was Avebury. It happened all the time.

Their ritual finished, the group sat down. A girl began to talk; the others listened.

"Place is crawling with weirdos." Dan sounded restless.

"You should know."

The girl speaker wore a purple skirt and a rainbow vest and her hair was short and red. She spoke clearly, and Rob listened, rolling after the pencil and making quick sketches of her on the corner of a page as she said, "Matty's drawn up the charts, and the stars are right. This is the day, and all the lines of power intersect on this very spot. I'm so glad you could all get here."

"They're cracked," Dan said darkly. "They think aliens make crop circles, when it's my uncle Pete's friend's brother from Winterbourne Bassett." He looked at his watch and pulled a face. "I've got to go. I'm on the evening shift."

Rob nodded, drawing the backs of the people. He pulled the backpack over, searching for the pastels. "See you tomorrow?"

"Probably. Come over anyway." Dan dragged himself up and loped off toward the pub, then turned and walked backward, pointing a threatening finger. "Get that job. Why should I be the only one to suffer?"

Rob grinned. He smoothed a few strokes of turquoise down for the back of a shirt. As he worked, the girl's words held his attention.

"We've known for months something was happening, that

someone is coming here. Long prophesied, long expected. A great soul, one of the Cauldron-born. A walker between the worlds, a sorcerer and a druid. We've done a lot of work, and we're sure he or she will be manifested here today, in the sacred circle. Matty thinks at seven o'clock exactly, when the moon rises over Silbury. So the plan is to meet them with joy."

"What if they're not in human shape?" someone asked.

The girl looked unconcerned. "They will be. We all know how powerful this place is. Our desire will draw them here, and they'll be what we need at this time."

Rob grinned. Dan would have loved this.

They waited. They lit incense sticks and lay on the grass and talked; a few seemed asleep or meditating. As the evening dimmed, the tourists in the great circle of stones began to seep away; coaches pulled out of the parking lot, cars full of tired kids turned toward home. The clouds that had gathered earlier began to thicken again; no one would see the moon rise through those, Rob thought acidly. Suddenly tired of sketching, he dumped the pastels in the tin and lay back, gazing up at the darkening sky through a haze of small dancing gnats. He should go home too. Maria would be gone by now. No one would be there at all. His mother would be at the nursing home with Chloe, and Dad still at the theater. It would be safe.

But he didn't move. The grass was lumpy; its discomfort nagged at him, but the effort of getting up was too great. The August day had been hot and humid; it seemed to have robbed him of all energy, and the twilight gathered as he lay there, the shadows of the stones lengthening vaguely in the purple light. Birds sang in a rowan bush. On the road the cars hummed, quieter than before.

He rolled his head. The rainbow people were still waiting.

For an instant then a flicker of the memory of the girl on the horse troubled him and he sat up, breathing the sandalwood mustiness of incense. He had no idea of the time, but it must be nearly seven because the group was getting ready, standing, calling the children together. A man started beating a small drum; the pulse of sound throbbed over the rough grass.

Rob looked around. Everyone else had gone. Apart from him, Avebury was empty.

Spots of rain began to darken the red cover of his sketchbook; he thrust it into the bag. He realized he was waiting around in curiosity to see no druid appear, to see the rainbow group's disappointment. The red-haired girl glanced over at him; then she and the others joined hands, crooning a low chant of three notes, over and over.

They were like people who predict the end of the world, he thought. Always sure, always waiting. Part of him smirked. But part didn't. The part that was desperate for a miracle since the accident.

Rain pattered. He pulled out his rain jacket and dragged it on, but the Barber's Stone kept the wind off, so he crouched there. There was no sign of the moon, just an ominous gray expanse of cloud, a wind flinging rain. The downs were blotted out. The night would be stormy.

The Cauldron people looked cold. They kept up the chant, but the wind whipped out their hair. Two of the kids gave up and ran off toward the tents. The red-haired girl looked again at Rob.

He met her eyes; she glanced away, spoke to another woman, who turned and stared at him too.

The church clock began to strike seven.

The group stood, expectant. He saw they had planted pennants and flags with symbols in the grass: a crescent moon, three cranes on a bull's back, a leaping salmon. A lot of the tribe were looking over at him now; Rob grabbed his bag and scrambled to his feet. Suddenly he was alarmed. Surely they couldn't think . . . Did they think it was him?

He turned, but the red-haired girl said, "Wait! Please!"

Rob froze. He spun around, embarrassed, wanting Dan. They were coming toward him, the tousled children, the man beating the drum, the frowsy women, even the dogs.

The red-haired girl was anxious, her voice taut. "We're waiting for someone. A being of great power, from far away, born again from the Cauldron. We know he's coming here, at this time, when all the stars are in alignment. There is a word we'll recognize him by, a secret word."

"It's not me!" Rob stumbled back. He raised his hands, shook his head. "Sorry. I don't know anything about stars. Still at school, me." He sounded stupid. He *wanted* to sound stupid.

Four strokes of the clock.

The people studied him. For a heartbeat he knew they despised him, doubted him, weren't sure. If Dan was here it would have been all right. Dan would have made it all into a huge joke. But the girl's look was desperate with hope. "Please look into your heart," she whispered, coming up to him. "Look into your heart and choose a word. Any word. It might be the one we know. No one else is here but you. It could be you, without your knowing."

It was crazy. He licked his lips, rain running down his hair. There was nothing to say, no word, no sound he could make that would satisfy them, but he had to say something, get away, break this circle of rain and faces and the insistent, terrifying clock crashing out the chimes, so he made himself whisper a word and the word that came out was *Chloe*.

The girl looked startled.

The name fell into huge silence. The bell stopped, and the drum. The only sound was the storm, stinging them all with its horizontal rain, whipping the girl's skirts, a gale that roared over the downs and hurled itself at the high grass banks, streaming in through the ancient gateways, around the leaning, silent stones.

And as if blown here by its fury, a bird fell from the sky.

It plummeted, a tiny swallow, exhausted, crashing into the grass beyond the top of the bank, and straight after it, talons down, a hawk shrieked, but the rain blurred and the bird was gone and the claws grabbed only mud.

The girl gasped. "It's him," she breathed. *"He's coming!"*

Wind roared. Out of the flattened grass something shot like a bolt. Rob saw a hare hurtle along the top of the bank, its great back legs thudding, and out of the place where the hawk had come down, the rain re-formed into the swift out-line of a slim dog that solidified as it streaked in arrow-straight pursuit.

The hare's eyes were wide with terror. Remorselessly the greyhound sped after it, teeth snapping.

The girl turned. "He's in trouble! Make the horseshoe!"

The hare leaped. It flung itself down the crippling slope into the ditch, falling and tumbling. Behind it the dog shape skidded, sending chunks of chalk flying.

The girl pushed Rob. "Help him!"

He had no idea who she was talking about. The group formed a hasty semicircle around the stone, open ends facing the deep ditch. They clutched hands; the drum began a rapid patter, and two men dragged the colored pennants up and rearranged them frantically, thrusting the pliant sticks into the ground, the thin silk flapping and slashing into streamers, red and gold as flames.

The hare crashed into the bottom of the ditch. Rob threw himself on his stomach, wriggled to the edge and looked down.

The ditch was flooded. Through its rain-spattered surface he could see grass, weeds, an object that became a fish. The fish dived deep with a flick of its tail; in the same instant the dog entered the water with an almighty splash.

Its shape streamlined with bubbles, lengthened, shivered. An otter sleeked by, its round head glistening.

"Now!" the girl screamed.

Rob scrambled down the slope; flung his hand into the water.

He caught something. Cold and slithery, scaled and slippery.

A fish.

It flexed, tightened, slid into a cold, soaked grip.

Fingers.

To his astonishment he realized a man was looking up at

him, struggling out of the water. Rob held tight, clutching the grass.

Soaked, breathless, the man heaved himself up, his eyes dark with exhaustion. He coughed, grabbed tighter. "Is that you, Prince?" he whispered.

The sleek rain-slashed pelt of the otter leaped. Its snarl was ferocious.

"Into the circle!" the girl yelled at Rob.

Rob pulled. The man made a desperate scramble and flung himself up the sheer wall of grass. He almost slid back; then Rob was stretching, hanging on with both hands. The stranger grabbed, a firm wet grip; Rob hauled and the man dug his feet in, clawing at the tussocks of grass. Above them the streamers crackled and burned; now they really were flames, their smoke whipped away by the wind, and the otter shape curled and slithered back down into the ditch, the sparks of the burning falling on it, making it yelp and howl.

"I've got you!" Rob gasped.

The man looked up at him. "I know," he breathed. "I know you have," and Rob saw his shape was strengthening as he coughed and climbed, the mud making him slip, the ditch wall a treacherous rampart, smooth and running with rain. And then he was at the top; he grabbed Rob's shoulder and dragged himself upright and stood breathless in the opening of the horseshoe, the banners on each side of him subsiding to streamers of silk and orange. He didn't look back.

But, scuffed and sore, his hands hot, Rob did.

The otter was watching. It looked up at him, its eyes blue. Then the rain blurred over it, and for a second Rob saw it shiver into a human outline, a woman's slim shape, her face spiteful and strange.

"Tell him I'll be waiting," she whispered. *"At the foot of the tree."*

Rain blurred the grass. When he blinked, the ditch was empty.

The stranger rubbed mud from his face. He looked worn, and all at once a little wary. "Thank you for bringing me in," he said, his voice oddly husky.

Bewildered, Rob shook his head. "Those animals—"

"There were no animals. Forget what you saw." He turned to the group.

The red-haired girl was in the center of the horseshoe. Without unlinking her hands, she gave a nod, and the people of the Cauldron stepped forward slowly, the children nudged by their parents. The ring closed around Rob. He and the stranger were trapped inside it.

It worried him, but the tall man seemed not to care. He folded his arms, as if preparing himself. His clothes were dark and unremarkable, but his face was narrow, his hair long on the nape of his neck, and touched with silvery gray, as if he should be old, though he seemed no more than thirty. A peculiar star-shaped scar slid over the end of one eyebrow, and his eyes were dark and quick, taking everything in. Around his neck, half-hidden inside his coat on a green cord, hung a small bag made of what looked like leather.

The girl stepped forward. "You're the one, aren't you?" She sounded awestruck.

The man smiled. Then he said quietly, *" 'I have been in many forms. A blue salmon, a stag, a roebuck on the mountain. The foam of the* ninth wave. A moth in a lantern, a harp note on the wind. Before I was born I lived. After I die, I will be born.'" He glanced around at them, their intent faces. "I'm a poet. Is that what you're waiting for?"

They eyed one another. Uneasily, Rob thought. He edged a step away from the stranger.

"Tell us your name," the girl said.

The man shivered, glanced down at the grass, the tiny plants growing at the foot of the stone. "I have many names," he said. "Why not call me Vetch?"

"That isn't the word we're waiting for."

"Word?" The stranger's calm eyes considered her.

The girl was impatient now. "Don't you know? Nine of us dreamed of a letter. Or it came in some way, in the ashes of the fire, in the whorls of wood. We put them together, rearranged them. They made a word. If you *are* the one we're waiting for, you should know it."

Vetch sighed. He was soaked and shivering uncontrollably, his arms wrapped around himself, the wind flapping his hair and coat. "I do know it. The word is the reason I've come, and that you're all here. The word is the time and the place and the danger." He looked around at them all, at Rob, at the darkness closing beyond the stones. Then he said wearily, "Couldn't we go somewhere a little drier than this?"

"First we need to know," the girl insisted. No one moved, or unlinked their fingers. Rain dripped relentlessly down Rob's neck.

The stranger coughed. "Poets know that words can be deceptive." He lifted his chin and, with an effort, drew himself upright. "But the word you want," he said quietly, "is *Darkhenge*."

N. NION: ASH

He said my name. Chloe. I don't know how he knows it.
There are no days anymore but he keeps the clocks ticking, and the
food on the long table is regularly changed. Sometimes it's salmon,
sometimes hazelnuts or apples. A bird sings somewhere in the
building—I've thought I heard it, but I can never find it.

The walls are not so thick after all. The trees scrape at them.
The trees seem alive, scrabbling up the stones, over the roofs, and
two of the windows I've found are already overgrown, smothered
with leaf.

I think the trees terrify him.

I've asked him about it. He won't say.

But I'm sure he's scared.

Don't be sorry at your catch.
Though I'm weak
My words hold wonders.

∽THE BOOK OF TALIESIN

Rob came in quietly and closed the door. He wheeled the bike into the garage, then went into the kitchen and opened the fridge. His heart was thudding from the ride back against the wind; he was soaked and shivering. Pouring orange juice, he drank it thirstily, leaning against the sink.

It was 8:35 PM.

The kitchen was quiet. Rain pattered on the windows and the tabby, Oscar, came in through the cat flap, eyed his empty plate and then Rob with a green glare. Rob couldn't take the guilt; he found a can and dumped cat food on the plate, then as he climbed the stairs, his father's key turned in the lock.

"What happened to you?" John Drew came in and stared.

"I got wet. On the bike."

"Just come in?"

He nodded. His father dropped into a chair and loosened his tie. "I don't suppose there's anything to eat?"

"Haven't looked."

"Mail?"

"On the table."

Upstairs Rob washed and changed, tossing his soaked jeans onto the heap of dirty clothes in the basket. There were so many the lid wouldn't go down. What was Maria doing all day? What had she left for dinner? Last week she'd taken huge offense at his father trying to be tactful. "I'm from Napoli!" she'd stormed. "I know about Italian cooking. What you know, eh?"

His father had had to admit he knew nothing, absolutely nothing, but it was too late. Since then she'd left them the blandest of British: soggy fish and chips, deadly steak and kidney. But her fits of pique rarely lasted more than a week, so there might be pizza. Her pizza was legendary.

He ran downstairs; his father said, "It's lasagne. We're forgiven."

Rob shrugged; he'd had it for lunch at the pub, but he didn't say anything.

The oven was lit; already the smell was making him realize how late it was. He set the table.

"Good day?" his father asked.

Rob hardly knew what to say. "So-so. Got some good studies at Avebury. Then it rained."

"Dan?"

"Mad. Thinks he's a seventies rock god."

His father laughed, checking the oven.

"What about you?" Rob muttered.

"Oh, some tiresome technical hitches with the stage. There's a touring opera production of *Tosca* due to open tomorrow and their battlements are too big for us." He wrapped the tea towel around his hands and juggled the hot plates to the table. "Get stuck in."

As they ate, Chloe's unspoken name lay between them, like the flowers in the vase on the table. It lodged in Rob's throat like an unchewed morsel. They lapsed into silence, and then dumped the dishes in the sink. While his father put the news on, Rob went upstairs. The door of Chloe's room was ajar.

He stared at it.

It was always kept closed.

Perhaps Maria had been cleaning in there, though she wasn't supposed to. It wasn't to be touched. His mother insisted.

Rob pushed the door, very gently, and it opened, making that familiar little creak on the bottom hinge. He went in.

It smelled of her. That sickly scent she always used to splash on, which he used to complain about, make out it choked him. The row of cuddly toys sat on the pillow, and posters of boy bands, already going out of fashion, were neatly aligned on the walls. Her clothes were in the wardrobe, but he didn't look in there. There were limits on how far his control could go, and he knew it, and never crossed them. Her school bag hung on the back of the door. There were books in there with her sums and essays in them. Her useless drawings.

It was far too neat for a thirteen-year-old girl. Before the accident the room had convulsed, clothes had come and gone in heaps on the chair, a pile that grew and shrank each week, each day; papers and diaries had opened and closed, books had had bookmarks travel through them; glitzy makeup and bath stuff in fancy bottles had been new, then spilled, half empty, gummy, thrown away; CDs had blared and strummed.

Now it was still.

As if a Pause button had been pressed, and the room held in flickering stasis, without sound or movement to disturb the faint dust on the sill. As if the room had become a chamber in that castle in the story Chloe had always liked when she was small, where the princess slept for a hundred years behind the briars and the tangled trees, just as she was sleeping now, while everyone else carried on, and got older.

He heard a car pull up, and went to the window, careful not to be seen. It was his mother, and there was someone with her—Father Mac, probably. Rob stepped back, and turned. Then he saw the photo of the horse. It was stuck on the side of the wardrobe, askew. A white horse, just like Callie. Like the horse at Falkner's Circle.

All at once, hearing the door open below and the voices, the memory of what he had seen that afternoon swept over him with its terrible, first jagged shock. He had seen his sister riding. It had been Chloe.

He sat on the bed, as if his legs had weakened.

How could it have been?

Something hard was under the covers. He put his hand

under the sheets and tugged it out. It was a journal, purple with stars on the front.

CHLOE'S DIARY it said on the front in felt pen. KEEP OUT. OR ELSE.

Elastic bands kept it shut.

For a long time he looked at it, the childish letters, the silly stars. Then he slid the bands off and let the book fall open on a page.

It's happened again. I drew a picture of Callie and he made fun of it. He snatched it off me and ran downstairs with it. Dan was there, and I could have DIED. I could hear them giggling about it. I hate him.

Rob hardly breathed. It hurt to breathe.

He remembered the stupid drawing, all out of proportion, and yes, he had snatched it and she'd been furious but . . . it had been a joke.

She always took things too seriously.

He snapped the book shut and shoved it back. Then he got up and went downstairs.

His father was watching *Newsnight* and talking to Father Mac; his mother was in the kitchen making a cup of tea. She brought it in and glanced at him quickly. "Hullo, sweetheart. I hear Maria is speaking to us all again."

Rob nodded. His mother looked tired, but as glamorous as ever. Her makeup was perfect, her pale blue cashmere top casual and expensive. He didn't know how she kept up the pretense. He said, "How's Chloe?"

Her eyes widened. Father Mac's hand made the briefest of pauses in its stretch for the tea. John Drew stared intently at the screen.

"The same." His mother kept her voice steady. "Her eyes flickered. Just after seven. They said it was a muscular spasm. Otherwise, the same."

They were silent; he nodded. Chloe was always the same. She had been the same—unmoving, her head lolling, fed intravenously—for three months and eight days. She would always be the same, which was why he couldn't ask anymore.

He turned away. "I might be getting a job."

The stillness shattered; they all moved at once. Father Mac took the cup, his father got up and went out, his mother flicked the television channels.

"A job?" the priest growled. "Who's that desperate?"

"As an archaeological artist."

"Sounds impressive. What do they pay?"

"No idea." He sat down. "Actually, I don't know anything about it, but it might be interesting."

Father Mac nodded, drinking. "Something a bit different for the portfolio."

"That's what I was thinking."

They were doing what they always did. Making a conversation up, acting it out before his parents. Reassuringly normal. His mother was the actress, but now she sat there tired and subdued, like an audience at a boring play. Their whole life was a play, a pretense at normality, he thought, getting up to see Father Mac out.

"You get straight to bed, Katie Mcguire." The priest took

the remote control in his big hands and turned the television firmly off. "Tomorrow's another day."

She looked up at him, her eyes red rimmed. "How many more days? How many, Mac?"

Gently, he shook his head. "Trust the Lord, Kate. Trust him. We'll get her back." He paused a moment, his gray-stubbled face hard, his eyes steady. Then he called, "God bless, John!"

Out on the porch, Rob breathed in the night air. The darkness of the garden was soft with smells: wet grass, lavender, honeysuckle. Bats flitted, tiny dark flutters around the roof. His godfather came and stood next to him, a big clumsy shape that took out a cigarette and lit it. The lighter made a sputter of sound, a cobalt blue flame. It threw shadows on the priest's face, moving hollows, darknesses. It would be good to draw him like that, Rob thought, to get all the edginess and danger that was in him.

The lighter went out; Father Mac started to walk down the drive. "So. Is this job at Avebury?"

"Not really. There's some sort of new dig toward East Kennet. I might not go—it's just an idea."

"You go." Mac turned at once. "If they think you've got something to fill your days, that'll help them. Remember our deal, Robbie. Problems to me, normal face to them. Untroubled. Supportive. Your mother's acting the biggest part of her life right now. Woman deserves an Oscar." He smoked rapidly, his weight crunching the gravel on the winding drive. Behind him the trees were dark against the sky. Just before the road he turned. "That reminds me. What's wrong?"

Rob grimaced. "Apart from the obvious, you mean?"

"Apart from that."

"Nothing."

"You look a bit . . . askew."

"What?"

Mac snorted. "Knocked sideways."

Rob smiled, alarmed. The big man was so sharp. It was as if he felt what you were thinking, picked up some sort of invisible vibe. For an instant Rob was ready to blurt it all out, about the girl on the horse who had been Chloe riding Callie, the horse that was dead now, that had been killed in the accident. For a second he was desperate to be reassured, to be told it couldn't have happened, that it wasn't real. But Mac wouldn't say that. Mac would smoke and consider and say something deep that would keep him awake all night, wondering. So instead he opened the gate and laughed. "Think I've joined a New Age tribe."

Mac groaned.

"People of the Cauldron, they call themselves. Waiting for a master to come down and lead them."

"He's already been. Hasn't anyone told them?" Mac ground the cigarette butt out and tapped Rob on the shoulder. "Don't you get mixed up with that guff. Well-meaning but totally confused, most pagans."

Going through the gate he took a few steps and turned. "Did he turn up?"

"Who?"

"This guru."

Rob shrugged. "Yes. His name's Vetch."

Father Mac looked at him a moment in disbelief. "Vetch. Very green."

"What?"

"It's the name of a plant. Better than Nettle, I suppose." He snorted. "Or Hemlock."

Watching the heavy figure wave and walk off up the village lane, Rob thought of the red-haired girl's wide, astounded eyes. Whatever *Darkhenge* meant, Vetch had spoken the word they had been longing for. They had crowded around the stranger, talking, questioning, demanding explanations, but he had said little else, smiling wanly and standing there swaying slightly, exhausted, as if at the end of some long journey. And all the time, even when the tribe escorted him toward their dilapidated tents and vans, he had looked beyond them at Rob. A secret look. As if they shared something.

Glancing down at his hand, Rob flexed the fingers, feeling again the man's wet, slippery grip. In the darkness he let himself think it.

The man had changed shape. Swallow, hare, fish. And so had the woman hunting him.

Wind stirred the trees, dripping spatters of rain, so he turned, and saw the lights were on in his mother's bedroom. Against the rise of the downs the house was big and dark, holding all its sorrow tight, reclusive in its vast garden, and beyond it the sky faded from palest lemon to cobalt blue in a watercolor wash without boundaries.

The bedroom light went out.

Rob hurried back. On the way he passed Chloe's old swing. The wind rocked it, gently, back and forth.

S. SAILLE: WILLOW

This window has a crack. There's a draft, very faint, coming from outside. Maybe if I can break the glass I can get some sort of message out.

The bird is in a cage. Like me. I hate that.

I won't eat anything.

All I can see is forest. The castle is in the middle. He calls it a caer.

I wonder if Mum and Dad and Mac are devastated without me.

I wonder if Rob's sorry now.

Anger grows in the deep places.
Deep, under the earth.

∞ THE BOOK OF TALIESIN

There was always a dig going on somewhere around Avebury. Every summer people came, usually students on some university course on the Neolithic or Bronze Age, cutting trenches out on the Beckhampton Avenue to find if it was really there, or investigating anomalies from aerial photos.

Silbury Hill was the strangest place in a landscape of strangeness. Rob could understand avenues of stone, and circles of them even; he could imagine processions, and dancing and, as Dan reckoned, bloodthirsty sacrifices, but with all the hills around why build an artificial one? Huge and conical, shaggy with grass, the vast mound dominated the downs. Even from here on the Ridgeway he could see it, peeping over the top of Waden, a platform in the sky. It could be a tomb, but no one was buried in it. It could be a place to observe the stars. He had no doubt that the Cauldron people would tell him it was the womb of the earth goddess. Getting back on the bike, he cycled over ruts, the bag on his back jolting. There were things you could never find out about the past. Digging up bits of antler could only tell you so much. The stories to explain them were all gone. Like what had made Callie rear up that day. What had flung Chloe off her back. As he came to the A4, he stopped, waiting for a gap in the traffic. They must have had artists, those Stone Age people. Decorating pots, making statuettes. Maybe a great artist designed Silbury. Maybe it had no purpose, but just was. Did art need a purpose?

He cycled across the road. Beyond it the Ridgeway dropped; it passed a line of burial mounds and then crossed the Kennet on a tiny, rickety bridge, leading him to the back lane of West Overton. He cycled faster now, on the tarmac.

It took ten minutes to find the dig. Here in the valley there were none of the wide, open views of the downland; hedges and houses and church towers gathered together, modern bungalows and cottages with satellite dishes turning their backs uneasily on the prehistoric, windy uplands.

Down a muddy lane with grass growing in its center he found a parked car, a few bicycles in the hedge. There was a gate, and he stopped the bike and looked through the bars.

At once a bearded man came out of a Portakabin. "Can I help?" It sounded more like a threat, Rob thought. He got off the bike.

"I heard you needed an artist. To draw finds and things." It sounded lame. He had no idea what the right name for the job was.

But the archaeologist just said, "Who sent you?"

"A girl. She said to ask for Dr. Kavanagh." He was glad he'd remembered the name.

The man turned. "Leave the bike."

Rob climbed the gate. The field was muddy, oddly so for chalk country, and as they walked he saw it led down into a hollow. At the bottom was the dig, but to his surprise a high metal fence had been erected all around it, so nothing could be seen.

"Wait here." The bearded man went inside, through a gate.

Rob glanced around.

It was eerily quiet. No rows of students troweling, no one taking photographs. A bird was chirping in the hedge, and beyond that somewhere a car droned down a distant lane. Wind rippled the edges of a plastic sheet. The rest of the field was deserted.

A woman came out from the metal fence. She was wearing blue overalls and a T-shirt, and had blond hair, tied back. She looked at him with hostility. "What girl?"

"I . . . don't know her name. She was a student."

"She had no business sending you here."

Rob blinked. "I'll go then. Sorry."

The woman frowned. "Let me see your work. I presume you've brought something."

He'd seen her before somewhere. It suddenly struck him that she might be Dr. Kavanagh, and the image he hadn't realized he had, of a middle-aged man in tweeds, vanished. Awkward, he took out a sketchbook and handed it to her.

She flipped through the pages. Rob tried to stand confidently. He hated people looking at his work, but he knew it was good. He was an accurate draftsman, he delighted in intricate drawings of anything that was complicated: machines, trees, buildings. At first the pages were ruffled quickly but he knew by the way she slowed, the way she gazed, that she was impressed. He lifted his chin a little.

"Well, yes. But you've had no training. We need sections, reconstructions, plans. Careful measurements, accuracy."

"I could learn." He licked his lips. "The girl said you were shorthanded."

Dr. Kavanagh closed the book and handed it back. She breathed deep, put her hands on her hips, and stared down at a muddy boot. Then she looked up at him, considering, and he saw her eyes were blue and clear.

"What's your name?"

"Robert Drew."

"Local?"

"Yes."

"Dependable? Not going off on holiday?"

"No," he muttered.

She was silent. Then she said, "Look, Robert, this project

is very important. It's also likely to prove controversial, so we don't want news of it getting out. If I trace any leaks in security back to you, you're off the site. Understand?"

He shrugged. Had they found treasure? Gold?

"We are short of people, though that's as I want it. There's not much money. Three pounds an hour, strictly cash. If anyone asks, you're just a volunteer. I can't be bothered with paperwork."

He could probably get more wiping tables, but then what he'd said to Dan was true. He had enough money. And somehow her reluctance made him more keen. "Okay."

She sighed, as if she still wasn't sure. Then she turned. "Come on."

The metal fence was head high. Behind it, he found a network of bewilderment: trenches, ridges of sliced soil, pegs and strings, tags with numbers stuck in the earth. The bearded man crouched in the center, and another student lay flat, scraping painfully at things Rob couldn't even distinguish from mud.

It was very disappointing.

"I'll give you a quick run-through," Dr. Kavanagh said briskly. "An aerial survey in the nineties showed up some peculiar crop marks in this field; a geo-phys study two years ago confirmed them. They showed a circular disturbance. Not so unusual in this landscape, but funds weren't forthcoming at the time to excavate anyway." She spoke rapidly, as if she were lecturing some group, her eyes darting over the site. He had a feeling she didn't miss much. "When we started to dig, though, everything changed. This hollow is possibly the most exciting thing in British archaeology for years." She pointed. "Notice anything about the soil?"

Rob swung the backpack off and dumped it; then he crouched, looking. He knew nothing about any of this, but it wouldn't hurt to seem keen. "It's the wrong color," he said.

She raised an eyebrow. "Meaning?"

"The soil around here is chalk. White, full of flints — I mean, I know this is near the river, but it's brown. Chocolate. Sort of burnt umber."

For the first time she looked at him with a flicker of interest. Then she said, "Yes. Well, it's actually a form of peat. A complete geological fluke, contained in an impermeable saucer of very hard rock, not at all like the chalk or local limestones. Not only that, but it's saturated with water, probably from a series of hidden springs rising under it. The conditions are totally bizarre for this area. That's what makes it so fascinating."

He stood, brushing his knees. There was nothing to say. It sounded totally boring to him.

She must have guessed that, because she laughed, a cool, mirthless laugh. "And look what we've found in it."

He looked. At first he couldn't make out anything at all, his eyes bewildered by the variety of trenches. And then, with the sort of shift he recognized from looking at optical illusions, the strangeness resolved into a shape inside the mess and disorder.

A circle.

A circle of black lumps, ridged, looking like coal. They

barely rose out of the peculiar clotted mud, and he had no idea what they were, but they made a wide ring, about ten meters across, and there were a lot of them. He counted quickly. Twenty-four.

"Buried stones?"

Her blue eyes considered him. "Not stone. Wood. Four thousand years old. Cut down and erected before iron was discovered, maybe before pottery on a wheel." She crouched, reaching out and rubbing one of the timbers with her hand; he could see now that the ridges were like the weathering on gateposts. "In fact before almost everything we take for granted—money, nations, wars, possessions. When men dreamed the earth was alive, when soil and stones talked to them, when the sun was a burning power to be placated, the stars told the time." Her voice had softened; she looked up at him. "So old, Robert Drew! And to be here still. Waiting for me to find it again."

For a moment she seemed quite a different person, younger, balanced on the edge of friendliness. And then she stood and brushed the mud from her knees and her voice was as cool and hostile as before. "You may as well start straight-away. We've taken photos, so I want a plan of the northwest section. Marcus will show you the ropes."

Marcus turned out to be the bearded one. "So she took you on!" he muttered, watching the woman stride back to the Portakabin. "Didn't think she would."

"Why is it so hush-hush?"

Marcus hauled the drawing board up and pinned graph paper on; it flapped in the breeze and Rob had to hold it down for him. "It's massive. She wants the credit. It'll make her career. Now, this is what you do."

It was complex, but hardly art. Measuring and drawing every tiny feature. But once he'd started, he found he settled to it quickly, squatting on a rickety stool, knees up.

The site was quiet. The other two—Marcus and Jimmy—chatted sometimes and he listened, but mostly the sounds were nothing but tiny scrapes of trowels, buckets, mud-clogged boots on the boards, the rattle of a filled wheelbarrow. The stillness of the afternoon came down around him like warmth; as his hand drew, his brain slipped into a dream state, vague and comforting. Until he remembered it was Thursday.

The dread was dull, and familiar. It came up from somewhere deep and he couldn't stop it; like spilled water over a drawing, it blurred and spoiled the afternoon's peace.

Tomorrow was his day for seeing Chloe.

"How are you doing on that?" Jimmy loomed over him. "We want to start taking the level down now, for the last hour or so."

"I've finished." He looked at the site, then back at his plan. The tops of the posts were thin outlines of black ink. They looked like crazy flowers.

"Great. You may as well help out then."

A shovel was put in his hand; he stared at it. "You mean dig?"

"Clever boy." He had already noticed Jimmy was the sarcastic one.

It was hot work, and harder than he'd thought. Marcus

mattocked the earth lightly, stopping and bending at anything interesting, then Rob and Jimmy shoveled the peaty soil into a barrow and Jimmy wheeled it off. When the layers changed color, infinitesimally sometimes, Marcus would crouch and scrape and pick out tiny fragments, his nose almost touching the soil.

Rob grew hot. His hands were sore on the smooth wooden handle. Pausing for a gulp of water, he saw he was spattered with the dark mud; it clotted his trousers and T-shirt, his sneakers were ruined with it.

Jimmy grinned. "Get you some overalls tomorrow."

Now they used trowels. Inch by inch, the surface came away. It smelled, a rich stink of fibrous rotting material, saturated, so that you could squeeze a handful till it dripped. There were few worms, but the stuff was packed with lumps and bone splinters. Clare Kavanagh had come out of the van and was watching; eagerly she jumped down and picked a piece out. "Antler," she said.

Rob straightened his aching back.

The antler was white, perfectly preserved. Clare's fine fingers turned the piece swiftly. "Look at the battered grooves here. They used it to dig with."

She handed it to him and his fingers closed around it. Who had dropped it here? he wondered. Who had been the last person to hold this?

"Boss!" Marcus came hurtling around the metal fence. "Car in the lane."

Clare turned at once, her ponytail whipping out. "Make sure it goes by. Wait, I'll come with you." She glanced around. "It's getting late. Pack up and make sure everything's covered. Set the water sprays up." As she went she glanced at Rob. "Be here at nine o'clock tomorrow. And remember, say nothing to anyone. It's just a few holes in the ground."

He frowned, scraping the mud from his shovel with a trowel. What did she think he was going to do? Ring the *Marlborough Chronicle*?

Marcus and Jimmy had gathered up the buckets and finds trays and wheelbarrowed them off; left alone, Rob turned the antler over in his hands.

Then he held it very still.

In the mud, just at the foot of the nearest of the wooden posts, something was squirming.

He stepped back, looked around for the others, but he was alone in the encircling metal fence. The ground was bubbling. Something was coming up from it. It seemed round, clumps of mud falling off it as it wriggled and twisted, and then its shape broke out into two flailing things that he thought for an appalling second were tiny arms. He dropped the antler and crouched, holding his breath.

It was a bird.

It was coming out of the earth alive, its feathers bedraggled and crusted with soil, eyes blinded by mud, beak gaping. He reached down and touched it in disbelief, and it panicked under his fingers, giving a squawk, fluttering.

He dug his fingers into the sodden peat around it, easing it out, holding it, feeling its heart throbbing through the clotted feathers. Under the dirt he could see its colors: blue and green, scarlet flashes on its wings. No species he knew.

"Rob! Give us a hand with these!"

"Coming." He didn't know what to do with it. The thought of showing it to them seemed strangely frightening. It was an impossible thing, a warping of reality. Instinctively, he held out his hands and opened them. "Fly!" he whispered. "Quickly!"

The bird panted. Its eyes were open now, looking at him. It unfolded a long tongue, then spread its wings, and he saw they were gaudy with red and blue. In an instant, with a startling flap, it had flown away, over the fence.

Rob turned back and stared at the soil.

Marcus put his head around the fence. "Did you hear? We need a hand with the sprays." He glanced at the mess on the smoothly troweled surface. "What happened there?"

Rob shrugged. He kept his voice very low. "I don't know," he said.

F. FEARN: ALDER

He saw the bird fly. I was going to tie a message to its leg but he was running up the corridor and I had to let it go quickly.

It scraped out through the cracked window and fluttered into branches.

He went quite still when he saw the broken glass. A branch reached in like a hand; even as we watched, it was growing inside, and the leaves on it were unfurling like they do in a speeded-up film.

He grabbed my arm and pulled me back.

The window splintered and fell in.

"The first caer is breached," he whispered.

Nine months was I carried
In Ceridwen's womb.
At first I was Gwion.
Now I am Taliesin.

∞ THE BOOK OF TALIESIN

Three strange things. The girl on the horse; Vetch; the bird from the ground.

Calmly, he considered them.

It might be the strain. He was under terrible strain. If he let it, it would crush him. He knew he hid from it behind layers of defenses.

Or it might be that these things were real, and he had seen them. Everyone knew Avebury was a focus for strangeness. He should ask Mac.

But it was Vetch who came into his mind, the man's dark look, his riddling words.

Vetch.

On the table beside him the flowers were fresh. They always were. The cut glass vase held roses today — white roses, barely out of bud, and the delicate smell of them filled the room. One perfectly round bead of water on a leaf caught his eye. It shone.

The nursing home was expensive, and fussy about details. The sunny room had pictures on its walls, calm, cool frames full of seascape, and a distant sunset over a forest. Nothing to alarm anyone. Rob had seen them so often he didn't really see them anymore, except for the line of forestry in the small oil by the door. Forestry against the sky. It was faintly disturbing. During the long hours he had sat here his eyes would slide to it, dreaming about the earthy smell under the trees, the deep coniferous glades. He had put up one of his own pictures too: a portrait of Chloe laughing. She'd always complained he never drew her; he'd had to do it from photographs. He remembered the hours in his bedroom, having to study her cheeky grinning face. The only way he had coped was by making it just a painter's exercise in color and technique.

His eyes moved around the room, looking for something else to rest on.

His mother's knitting. A great pile of red wool. He had no idea what she was making; she used it to give her hands something to do. A crucifix on the wall. That new, unworn dressing gown.

Always, though, his gaze came back to the bed.

Chloe lay on a mound of pillows. Over the months her

hair had grown; it was below her ears now. She wouldn't like that. She liked her hair short, what Dad used to call her Peter Pan look, all spiky bits. Long hair made her look older, but then she *was* older. It would be strange for her, to wake up and find she was older.

That three months had vanished.

There were tubes to the veins in her arms, but not to her mouth and nose, because she breathed by herself. That was what puzzled the doctors. At first they'd kept her on a ventilator, but his mother had made them stop. "She can breathe. Let her breathe."

There was brain activity too, jagged peaks on the monitor. So she just looked as if she was asleep, as if she was the princess in that story, sleeping for a hundred years while outside everything went on as normal. Buses rumbled by, school terms ended, exams happened, birthdays, summer holidays.

He frowned. Her birthday. "What a fiasco that was!" he said aloud. They were supposed to talk to her, because it would help, the nurses said. They said she heard it. Rob didn't know if he believed that anymore.

He got up and wandered closer. "Remember the cake? Just there? Fourteen candles and the smoke alarms went off. Nearly got the place evacuated."

He laughed harshly. "But you know Mum. Has to make a fuss."

Everybody else, he knew, would have preferred a few cards, flowers, some music tapes in fancy paper, because what other present could you give someone who didn't move or talk and who might not even be there anymore? But his mother had wanted a party, because she never gave up. It had been appalling. Alone with Father Mac in the car on the way home, he had curled up in the dark on the backseat and Mac had let him, not saying a word, just letting him be. They had both been silenced by it. His mother's terrible happy chatter. By the unwrapped clothes, the new watch, the cell phone.

He rolled the bedside drawer open now and looked down at the phone.

It was kept charged. If she woke up when Mum wasn't here, it was for her to ring home, straightaway.

"She'll never give up waiting, Chloe. If you only knew what it's like now, at home. She's turning down so much work—anything in America, anything that takes her away. She's still doing the cops series, and there was talk of a film, but they won't do it without her." He turned and sat down on the bed, taking his sister's hand. It was cool, and oddly soft.

"Every time the phone rings, she jumps. She doesn't care about the fans, or the interviews, not like it was before. It's all acting now."

Holding her hand. It wasn't something he'd do if she was awake. If she stirred now he'd drop her fingers fast, because she'd be astonished and say something sarcastic. She was always saying cutting things to him, he realized. He wanted to say sorry about the picture of Callie, but that would mean telling her he'd opened her journal. She'd go mad. If she could still hear.

Abruptly, he put her hand down and stood. His hour was

up. He could go with a clear conscience now, but there was something he had to say first.

He turned and looked down at her, the still girl in the pink pajamas, the new watch ticking time away on her wrist.

"I saw you. It was you at Falkner's Circle. I know it was you, Chloe, so don't tell me it wasn't." His voice was angry; he let it be. Lately he was often angry with her. "What's happening? Are you dead and was that your ghost? Has your soul got out of your body and is wandering the downs? All sorts of odd things are starting to happen, and I don't like it, Chloe. You've got to stop it! Are you listening to me? *Listen to me!*"

He was yelling at her. His own fury shook him, and then out of nowhere came a sudden certainty that she heard him, that she would open her eyes now, sit up, yawn. He didn't breathe, waiting, knowing it would be now.

Now.

But she stayed the same. He unclenched his fists, breathed out. That old fantasy. It kept coming back.

The door opened and the big nurse, Mel, put her head around. "Everything okay?"

"Fine." They had probably heard him shout.

"Time for Chloe's bed bath."

"All right," he said. "I'm just going." At the door he turned back and looked at his sister. "I know you don't really hate me, Chloe. Do you?"

There was no answer. After a moment, he walked out.

∞

He bought a can of Coke in a newsagent's on the main road and leaned against the wall, drinking from it. The warmth of the sun was the best thing he had ever felt; he realized he was chilled, that sweat had dried on his back. He pulled out his sunglasses and put them on. The world went a rather crazy yellow.

"Hey. Want a lift?"

A car had stopped at the traffic lights; it was old, a little dirty. The door swung open and a girl leaned over, her red hair bright. "We're going back to Avebury. Jump in."

The girl from the Cauldron tribe. He emptied the can, dumped it in the bin on the lamppost, and slid into the car.

She and another girl were in the front. "Sorry about the mess."

The car smelled of perfume. Crystals hung on the windshield, and the music coming from the speakers behind his head sounded Indian maybe. World stuff.

"My name's Rosa." She changed gear. "This is Megan."

"Hi. Rob."

She turned the music down. "Vetch said we'd see you."

Rob stared at the back of her head. "What?"

She grinned at the girl next to her, a closed smile. "He's such an amazing person. He said you'd be along, because you're part of it. You pulled him into the sacred circle."

Rob said, "Oh. Right." He leaned back and stared out of the window, wishing she'd turn the music up again so he wouldn't have to talk. He should have got the bus. If Dan found out, he'd never hear the end of this.

They had crossed the M4; now the road swung through Wroughton, with its pretty green and millstream. Passing the Three Tuns, the other girl said, "You live in Avebury?"

"Just outside."

"Lucky. This is such a special landscape."

He said nothing; Rosa glanced at him in the mirror. "I expect you think we're a bit crazy. We're not really hippies, you know. I'm a medical student. Meg's a mum. All the group come from different places, some from Europe. This is the first time we've met."

He wasn't interested but he said, "Because of dreams?"

She shrugged. "No ordinary dream. It was incredibly vivid. I was walking in the sea, ankle deep, and there was this beach and I had it all to myself. The sky was gray, as if it was going to rain, and there was a wind whipping my coat out. It wasn't like a dream. I could feel it."

He nodded. The car droned up the sudden, steep side of the Marlborough downs.

"Then I looked into the sea. And I saw the sand wasn't grains at all but letters, tiny, tiny letters. Billions of them. All the same. D."

"D?"

She laughed. "Weird, or what? So I put it on the group Web site. The other messages came back almost instantly. Nine of us had had the same or a similar dream. With some it was in a wood, or in a room or a building. But there was always one letter of the alphabet that was featured. So we put them together. They made the word Vetch knew."

"Darkhenge," Rob said. And as he said it he went cold with sudden realization and dismay. *"Darkhenge!"* He bit his lip. "I think . . . Do you know what it means?"

"Hang on. We're picking him up here."

A bridle path. Like the rest of them it came down from the Ridgeway, the ancient road, distant here, high on the crest of the downs. As soon as the car turned in and the engine was switched off, the silence of the wide country surged through the open windows. Megan opened the passenger door and swung her legs outside, looking up the track. "Here he comes."

Vetch was walking toward them. He still wore the dark clothes, despite the heat of the afternoon. On either side of the white track the fields were drifting acres of golden crop, the wind causing shivers that changed shade and tone. The sky was vast, a dome of blue air.

Vetch waved. Rob heard the scuff of his boots, saw the dust of the chalk rise. He climbed out of the car and leaned against it, waiting.

The dark-haired man came up and stopped. "I told them you'd be back."

Rosa gave him a bottle of water; he opened it and drank gratefully, looking up at the crest of the downs. "I've always loved this place," he said quietly. "It's very good to be ending things here."

"Listen." Rob was uneasy. "What does *Darkhenge* mean?"

Vetch drank again. Then he stoppered the bottle deliberately. "I think you already know that, Rob. What's more, I think you've seen it."

"I don't—"

"Don't lie to me." Vetch looked up at him quickly, eyes dark. "It's down there in the valley, isn't it? Near the river. I can feel it emerging. I can feel it coming back out of the earth."

The two girls were listening intently. Rosa said, "The whole group ought to hear this."

Vetch nodded. "Agreed. But does Rob want to come?"

He shrugged. He did and he didn't. If Dan saw him with this crowd he'd never hear the end of it.

"Shall we go?" Vetch gestured at the car. He had long, rather delicate fingers.

Rob stood his ground. "How did you know I'd seen it?"

Vetch came past him and opened the car door. He sat wearily on the hot leather seat, propped one foot up on the dashboard, and drank again, smiling out at the fields of barley.

"A little bird told me," he said quietly.

The
Crane–skin
Bag

U. UATH: HAWTHORN

We traveled all night, through the forest. The carriage
bounced along rough tracks. The forest was dark and the trees
crowded close, and far back there was some sort of murmur, as if
the wind blew, but not here.

I got the feeling he wanted to apologize, but he never spoke.
He kept looking back, over his shoulder.

Then there were lanterns in the trees. "This is it," he said.
"The second caer. You'll be safe here, Chloe."

I wish he'd take that silly mask off.

Terrible the anger of the goddess who pursued me.

~ THE BOOK OF TALIESIN

They drove down to Avebury in silence, apart from the drifty music, then turned up Green Street through the great opening in the bank and pulled in under the trees. The lane was quiet and leafy. As Rob had expected, a few tents were pitched in the copse, the smell of a fire acrid in the heat.

"Are you all camping out here?"

Rosa laughed. "Most of us like a little more comfort. I'm in a B and B. Some have camper vans and things."

He looked at Vetch. "What about you?"

The man smiled his enigmatic smile. "Never mind. Come and tell us about the henge."

There was hot coffee; it smelled rich and tasted better. When Rosa had got everyone together, they all sat around drinking and looking curiously at Rob. He had a desperate desire to make an excuse and go, had just summoned enough courage to do it when Vetch held up a hand for silence.

When they could hear the breeze in the leaves above them he said, "Rob has seen Darkhenge. Tell the group about it, Rob."

He frowned. "It's supposed to be secret."

"Not from us. We already know." Vetch had taken the small skin bag from around his neck and placed it beside him. His coat, Rob noticed, was worn and frayed at the sleeves.

The group waited, expectant. So he shrugged and breathed out and said, "There's a circle, and it's made of wood. Ancient timbers. They're all really excited about it. They haven't excavated very far down yet, so you can only see the tops of the posts. I don't know how far down it goes." He looked up. "Is that what you mean by Darkhenge?"

Vetch smiled, but didn't answer. One of the men said, "A timber henge? Intact? That's incredible."

"It's a freak, the woman told me. Trapped layers of water have preserved it. I told you, they can't believe it themselves. The woman in charge is called Dr. Kavanagh—"

He stopped. Beside him Vetch had taken a small, sharp breath. "*Clare* Kavanagh?"

"Yes."

"You know her?" Rosa asked.

Vetch scratched his cheek ruefully. "Once I knew her."

"She's ferocious. If she thought I was telling you — "

"Don't worry, Rob." Rosa tapped his shoulder. "There's no one here who'll say it was you. You have no connection with us."

"Unless someone sees me."

"How long will it take?" One of the men, Tom, was looking at Vetch. "For them to dig it out?"

The poet shrugged. "One, two weeks. The timbers will need to be kept wet; they'll have to work quickly. Clare won't waste time. It will be cleared, and then . . . removed."

"Removed?" Rosa looked appalled. Vetch glanced at her, his star-shaped scar bright in the sun. "I'm afraid so. Archaeology, in the end, is destruction. To discover what the henge is, to find its date, the way it was made, they will break it down. Once open to the air it will rot, so they'll feel they must preserve it. The timbers will be hauled out and taken to some tank somewhere and treated. You know that's what happens."

"They should leave it where it is," Tom growled. "Where it belongs."

Vetch spread his fine hands. "Indeed, it would do them more good. Because the things they will learn are useless things. What does a date mean? Time circulates in our minds, nowhere else. The purpose of the henge lies in the place it is and the thing it is. The henge is a gateway. It can't be unlocked with spades."

"And you know all about it?" Rob said quietly.

Vetch looked up at him, and the smile had gone. *"Oh yes. I know."*

In the silence that followed Megan said, "No wonder they want it kept quiet. There'd be media frenzy, in Avebury of all places. It's crawling with all sorts of New Age groups, neopagans, local activists, dowsers. . . ."

Rob closed his eyes in dismay. "There goes the job. I was just getting to enjoy it."

"But you don't need it. Or so you said." Vetch's voice was quiet.

Rob opened his eyes and looked at him in alarm. "How do you know what I said or didn't say?" It was to Dan he'd said that. Before he'd ever seen Vetch.

"Because I've drunk from the Cauldron, Rob, and nothing is hidden from my sight." Vetch opened the bag slowly. "I have eaten the hazels of wisdom. Talking of which . . ." He drew out a handful of small nuts—hazel, Rob thought, with the leaves still on—placed them on the ground and said, "Help yourselves."

Two or three of the group looked at one another. Hands stretched out. Rob said, "I should be going."

Vetch popped one of the nuts in his mouth and chewed. He was leaning against the trunk of a tree; its branches made a cool green shadow on his face and eyes.

"First, I need a favor from you. I want to see the henge, Rob."

"No way—"

"Just to see it. You can tell me where it is but I assume there are security precautions."

"A fence," he said reluctantly.

"Electrified?"

"I don't think so."

"Is that all?"

"Two of them sleep there, in a van. Marcus and Jimmy. Jimmy's got a dog." He shook his head, suddenly annoyed. "The fence is locked and I haven't got a key. If you want to go there, go on your own. Leave me out of it." He stood up, aware all at once that time had passed, that the heat of the day was cooling. Vetch watched him, his eyes shadowed and calm.

"And is it only the bird, so far, that has emerged?"

Rob swallowed.

Amused, Vetch laughed; Rob sat again, slowly. Then he said, "That bird. How did it happen? I saw it come out of the earth, alive. No species I've ever seen." He shook his head. "Things are happening . . . I need to ask you . . . someone . . ."

"I know." Vetch glanced around. "You see, everyone. It begins, as I said it would."

"Where did the bird come from?"

"From Annwn."

The word meant something to the group; nothing to Rob. "Where's that?"

But Vetch glanced at Rosa. Instead of answering he said, "I think Rosa has a question to ask you."

Startled, she stared at him. "Master—"

"I told you, you must call me Vetch," he said softly. "Ask the boy. It's troubling you."

Rosa frowned. She rubbed her nose and sighed. Then she said, "I'm sorry, Rob, but he's right. Who is Chloe?"

"What?"

"When I asked you to choose a word, you chose that one. Chloe."

"She's my sister," he said shortly. He scrambled up, angry now, knowing they had pierced an invisible wall he kept around himself. It was Vetch he was angry with, Vetch who looked at him with that infuriating dark look, who never answered his questions except with others. "Why not ask him?" he snapped. "Your druid . . . he's the one who claims to know bloody everything."

It was so silent he could hear a bird wheezing out three notes of a song high in the windy hawthorn.

Vetch stood up. He stepped past the guttering fire and the sprawled listeners and came up to Rob, his eyes steady. Rob stepped back. He did it without thinking, and that made him angrier. But before he could swing away Vetch had put his hand out, his narrow, long hand, and had touched him lightly on the chest.

Rob didn't move.

"One of the poet's gifts is the *imbas forosnai*," Vetch said softly. "The drawing out of knowledge. For instance, I know now where you live; that your mother is an actress and your father the stage manager of a small theater in Oxford. I know that you see the world in colors and shapes as an artist sees it. I know that Chloe is indeed your sister, or she was, because three months ago she fell from her horse at Falkner's Circle."

Behind him the group was silent, stiff, as if with embarrassment or wonder. "And since then," Vetch murmured, his voice husky, "she has lain between waking and sleeping, between life and death. She has fallen into Annwn. The Unworld."

Rob pulled away. The trees were crackling. An electric tingle seemed to be crawling all over his nerves and scalp. Vetch stepped after him, close up. "And I know how that makes you feel, all your weary hours, your dreams, the long silences in the house, the unspoken grief like a weight no one can take from you."

They looked at each other. *"No,"* Rob said tightly. *"No you don't."*

Tension was brittle. Then Vetch smiled his slow smile. "Maybe not."

Instantly, like an invisible wave, weariness seemed to come over him; he almost staggered, and Rob's hand shot out automatically.

Rosa leaped up. "Master . . ."

"I'm fine." He rubbed his face wearily. "Thank you, Rosa." Then he looked up. "Tomorrow night we'll come. At midnight. It will be easier if you can get hold of the key to this fence."

"I can't."

Vetch nodded. "Be careful of Clare Kavanagh. She's full of anger. And ambition."

He turned and went and sat down by Rosa.

Helpless, Rob stared at them all. "There is no way," he said fiercely, "that I'm getting any key."

Vetch took a hazelnut and tossed it to him. "You will, Rob." He lay back against the bank and closed his eyes. Quietly he said, "To find Chloe, you would do anything."

Walking furiously down the village street, he almost collided with Dan.

Dan took one look at him and said, "Come to my place? I've got this new recording of—"

"No. Thanks." He looked around absently. Then he went into the churchyard and sat on the grass. Dan came after him.

"What's wrong?"

"It's Friday. What do you think's *wrong*?"

Dan pulled a face. "Sorry. I forgot."

"I wish I could."

"We could go weirdo-watching."

"I've seen you. Anyone else is an anticlimax."

"We could go to the flicks."

Rob shrugged.

"Pub?"

"I'm going home." He scrambled up. "For a change."

"How's the job?"

Rob scowled. "Okay. It's drawing, of a sort. No creativity in it though. Pared down. Emotionless. Just hundreds of tiny lines, showing what's there." He shrugged. "They don't let me draw what's not there. That's what real artists do."

Dan pulled a baffled face. "Is it? No wonder I failed the GCSE. So what are they digging up? More stones?"

He didn't want to talk about it now. "Too early to tell." Taking his hands out of his pockets, he found the hazelnut in one, and threw it hard at Dan, who caught it one-handed and yelled, "Hey!"

"See you Sunday."

He had already walked three paces when Dan said, "Where did you get the hazelnuts?"

Rob was still. Then he said, "From Annwn."

D. DUIR: OAK

There seems to be a series of fortresses, each deeper in the wood. He calls this the second caer. Glass Castle.

It's brighter than the last. In fact the walls are nothing but a greenish shimmer so I can see that the slopes that were grassy yesterday are already thick with saplings.

Last night (though it's always night) he went up on the roof and stood looking east for a long time.

"What's wrong?" I asked, coming behind.

He rarely answers my questions, but he did this time. "A hole is opening in the world. Birds and bats are leaking out. Power is leaking out."

"When are you going to let me go?" I demanded.

His eyes were puzzled through a new, oak-leaf mask.

"Go where?" he said.

I fled in raven's shape,
As a fast frog.
I ran from my chains with despair,
A roebuck in deep woods.

∞ THE BOOK OF TALIESIN

"Well, something must have made it!" Clare Kavanagh folded her arms in fury. "Could a fox have got in here?"

"I don't know!" Marcus looked cowed. "Do foxes dig?"

"Of course they do," Jimmy muttered.

The blond woman stared around. "If it was coin hunters waving metal detectors, they're wasting their time."

"No one's come over that fence, boss. And Max didn't bark all night."

"He went to the door though," Marcus said quietly. "Remember? Made a sort of growl."

Behind them, Rob pinned a new sheet to the drawing

board, keeping his head down. No one took any notice of him; he wondered if they even realized he'd turned up this morning. Then he moved so he could see the hole too. "More like something came out than dug in," he said quietly.

Clare gave him a look of disgust. Then she said, "Let's get on. Switch the sprays off. We've wasted too much time already."

It was Saturday, but they worked hard. When there was nothing left to plan, Rob got down in the henge and dug with them carefully around the dark timbers with a fine-pointed trowel. For hours he worked, absorbed in the delicate scraping of granules of soil, their infinite shades of browns and golds and ochers, all the earth colors folded and laid so finely on top of one another, each tiny layer that his trowel cut away a hundred years of time, of people living and dying, of wars and empires. Vetch had said time was a circle in the mind, but it was here too, lying dormant, packed hard in the stinking, drying, fly-buzzed remnants of the peat hollow. As he crouched and lay, sat and knelt, Rob felt the textures of the past grime his skin. There were clotted masses of fiber that he picked out and prized apart, finding minute leaves of long-dead plants and insects still perfect in the de-oxygenated watery mass. He became absorbed in the work, just as he did with painting something with a very tiny paintbrush, his face close to the surface, cleaning the fissured edges of the timber posts, the ancient ridges smooth and hard as rock.

Around him the others worked, Jimmy with headphones on, Clare and Marcus talking occasionally in undertones, Max the Alsatian lying out in the field and lifting his head whenever a car purred up the lane.

By lunchtime, when Rob straightened wearily to aching knees, it was clear that the timbers were not isolated from one another. As the soil between them was removed it could be seen that one side of each was shaven; that they joined one another; made a wall, a black fence. Only in one place was there a gap, obviously the entrance, where Marcus was scraping. There had been no finds. No more bits of antler bone, no gold, no charcoal, nothing.

"There must be an object in the center."

Rob looked around. Clare Kavanagh was standing at his elbow. Today her blond hair was dragged back in a ragged plait, her ill-fitting blue overalls worn through at the knees. As she stared out thoughtfully, he thought she looked older than he'd realized. Tiny crow's-feet were starting to wrinkle her skin. She turned; Rob jerked his gaze away. But all she said was, "You look at things very closely, don't you?"

He shrugged.

"So do I." She turned back. "The central deposit is the key. The ditch and the timber fence were built around it, built tight, so no one could see in, or get in. Only the elite. The priests, warrior-kings, whoever."

"The sorcerers," Rob muttered.

She shrugged, absorbed. "Maybe." Then as if the

word triggered something, she said suddenly, "Who were those people I saw you with in Avebury yesterday?"

He froze. "Yesterday?"

"Yes. I thought you said you were going to some hospital."

"I did. I was." He sounded panic-stricken, he thought, so he pulled himself upright. "They were friends. They gave me a lift back." *And what business is it of yours?* he wanted to add, but she was gazing at him now, a thoughtful scrutiny.

"I thought . . . There was a man in the front seat. Dark-haired. I thought I recognized him."

"Vetch," he said boldly.

She frowned. "Wrong name. Does he live around here?"

"I suppose so."

"If it's him . . . ," she said, almost to herself. Then she rounded. "Look, Rob, I can't tell you who to see but I'm warning you, if people find out about this dig, then you're the one I'm going to be blaming."

"That's not fair," he snapped.

"Maybe, but Marcus and I go way back and he vouches for Jimmy."

"Others know! That girl in the pub!"

"My students. They won't cross me." She stepped up to him. "Don't you, either. This is big for me. Most archaeologists never ever in all their careers come across something as amazing as this. This time no one's going to get in my way."

She gave him a hard look and stepped back down into the central area. "Go and put the kettle on."

In the dingy trailer, he filled the kettle and banged it on the stove in fury. She couldn't speak to him like that! He didn't need her stupid job and he couldn't care less about her stupid career. Unable to find the matches, he slammed the drawer in disgust and leaned on the drain board, glaring out of the tiny window. Then he turned around.

First he closed the trailer door and slipped the catch. Next he went into the office. There was a desk with papers all over it, a finds tray with pieces of bone, a scatter of tools. Invoices and bills were pinned to notice boards. Near them was a hook and on it were keys.

Rob glanced out the window. No one had come through the metal fence. It struck him for a moment that the metal fence was doing the same job as the wooden timbers had done centuries ago: keeping the unwanted people from seeing the mysteries inside.

He turned back, and took down the keys.

The one for the gate was large, easy to find; he'd seen Marcus open up with it in the mornings. But if he took it, they'd know.

He put the key back with the others and opened a drawer. Papers. Pens. A box of clips, erasers, pencil stubs. A brown manila envelope with THURSTAN'S LOCKSMITHS. That shop was by the bus station in Swindon. He tipped the envelope up, and a key slid out.

It was the spare.

"Rob! Can you bring me some plastic bags?"

Jimmy had his head around the fence; instantly Rob

shoved the key in his pocket, the envelope to the back of the drawer, and slid out into the kitchen. "No problem!" he yelled, grabbing the matches from the table and cracking one into blue flame. "And the tea's nearly made."

All afternoon the key seemed heavy in his pocket. When he managed to forget about it, it stuck in him as he knelt or stretched stiff legs. Clots of peat fell from his sleeves, trouser knees, from the silver foil Maria had put around his packet of sandwiches, from the handle of the chipped tea mug. His hands were black, his nails clogged. As his temper cooled, guilt clogged him too.

He began to wish he hadn't taken it. Could he get it back without anyone seeing? Or maybe it would just be easier to tell Vetch he hadn't been able to get it, he thought. But the poet had an uncanny way of knowing things. About Chloe, for instance.

Hour by hour, the soil level dropped. By four o'clock the timber fence was a meter deep and still they hadn't found the bottom. Crouched in the heat, Rob smelled the enclosing rotting smell of peat; he pulled out a lump with his hands and it cracked open.

A small, gleaming beetle lay within, perfectly preserved.

He smiled, and touched it, and then almost crushed the thing with a convulsion of shock.

The beetle moved. It crawled onto his wrist and stood poised.

It uncreased small wings and flew away.

Rob looked around.

There were hundreds of them. He could see them now. They were crawling out of the buried henge, out of the heaps of soil in buckets and barrows. The air was alive with tiny whirrs and flashes of iridescent carapace, bronze, gold, green as shiny foil.

Like the bird, like whatever had made that hole, they were *emerging*.

"Do you think," he said later to Father Mac, sitting in the presbytery garden picking soil off his hands, "that Chloe will ever wake up?"

The priest's large sandaled feet crossed at the ankle. Lighting a cigarette, he flicked a glance at Rob. As usual, he showed no surprise. After a while he said, "It's possible. At least things will change." He shook the match out. "Chloe's condition is a mystery. None of them understand it, even that specialist your mum flew in. It's a freak situation."

"That word again."

"Word?"

"Freak." He gave a sharp, painful laugh. "She's preserved. Like the timbers in the henge. Not living, not dying."

Father Mac said nothing for a moment. Then he leaned forward and blew smoke into the roses. "Feeling the strain, son?"

"Maybe."

"There are two options, you know that. She wakes—and

that gets less likely as the days go on. Or she deteriorates. Brain activity stops."

"And they remove the feeding tube? Mum would never—"

"She may have to."

"*You* say that?"

The priest gave a heavy shrug. "Rob, if the brain is dead then the time has come. The Church believes death should not be artificially withheld—you know that. As for Katie"—he frowned—"when—if—the time comes, she'll do what's right."

Rob didn't want to answer. It was as if they weren't talking about a person, about cheeky, stroppy Chloe, sentimental over cats, bossy with her friends, who wouldn't eat ice cream because it rotted your teeth, but spent a fortune on sweets. He fingered the key in his pocket, turning it over, until he realized what it was. Father Mac smoked silently. Around them the summer garden darkened, smelling of lavender, and of the candle on the table that the moths dipped into and singed themselves against until Father Mac reached out and snuffed it with his thick, strong fingers. "Get home to bed," he growled. "Your mother needs you."

Rob said, "I found Chloe's diary."

Mac was silent.

"She'd written this thing . . . about me. About me pinching one of her drawings and making fun of it. I'd forgotten all about it. She sounded really gutted."

Mac looked out at the roses. Then he said, "Don't get it out of proportion. Little girls of that age—"

"But I'd forgotten. What else have I forgotten?"

"You had arguments. It's normal."

He nodded. Unconvinced.

The downs were silent. As Rob cycled along the road into Avebury, there was no traffic, though the pub windows were lit. Under the moonlight the great stones stood in their extraordinary cumbersome stillness, vast gray shapes. Their outlines were strange against the early stars, revealing faces and sharp noses, frowning brows. He turned past the church, the tires of the bike skewing loud against dry loose stones, down the silent street lit by one faint lamp, along the high wall, around the corner and over the tiny gurgle of the Winterbourne, almost dry. Beneath the bridge a disturbed duck rustled in the weeds.

The lane to his house was very dark. On each side untrimmed hedges reared, walls of shadow. He rode more slowly. Then he stopped, balanced with one foot on each side of the tipped bike, his breath loud.

Someone was standing near the gate.

He could see only a dark figure leaning against an oak tree there. But he knew who it was.

"How did you find out where I live?" he breathed.

Vetch straightened. His face was a mask of shadow and green glimmer. "As I told you, one of the poet's gifts. One of the three hot splashes of the Cauldron." He held up his right hand and turned it over; Rob saw that the back was burned: three fearsome scars lacerated the white skin. "Knowledge costs," Vetch said quietly. "As you're finding out."

He tipped his head, looking at Rob. "You've got the key." It wasn't a question.

"Yes. Look —"

"Did she threaten you?" Rob nodded. "That's because she feels threatened. She senses me out here, waiting." For a moment he seemed almost sad; his smile barely there. "Knowledge has to be stolen, Rob. Snatched from under the eyes of the wise, from the Muse's Cauldron, as Prometheus stole fire from the gods. They punished him. For eons his guts were torn out by an eagle. You know something about that."

Rob flipped the bike pedal up and rode past him, into the gateway. "I've changed my mind," he said firmly. "I'm not getting involved. I want it all to stop."

"It won't stop." Vetch came up behind him. "Whatever you or I do, the henge is emerging. But it's a chance. A gateway." Rob heard his voice alter; the calmness went out of it. "What is it, Rob, you want most in all the world?"

"You know what." Rob turned.

Vetch nodded. The starlight lit the star mark on his brow, and it shone, silver bright. "Then bring the key, at midnight. Because for me the henge leads home. And for you, it's the way to the place where Chloe is."

Rob's indrawn breath almost choked him. *"You're crazy,"* he whispered.

But halfway up the stairs he was stopped by a jolt of memory that went through him like pain, so that he shivered and gasped out loud.

He had remembered where he had seen Clare Kavanagh before.

The hawk, the dog, the otter, the woman.

Hunting Vetch into the circle.

T. TINNE: HOLLY

Now this caer *is surrounded too. The outer walls were meshed first; then we heard a crash and the gates fell; a great trunk bursting through the glass.*

He caught my hand and made me run with him up the wide stairs, all made of crystal.

"It's no use," I said, breathless. "The trees will get inside. Why are you so afraid of them?"

I remember reading somewhere that if you're kidnapped, you talk to him. Get to know him. You get under his skin.

He sat on the top step and rubbed his hand through his hair. "Never mind. I have a secret passageway to get us out."

I folded my arms. "Is the mask because you think I might recognize you?"

He shrugged.

I grinned. Mac would be proud of me. I'm beginning to work out a plan.

The green holly
Was a fierce fighter;
His dark spines defended,
Piercing palms.

∞ "THE BATTLE OF THE TREES"

R̶ob didn't undress.

He lay on the bed and stared up at the ceiling.

In the next room, he guessed, his mother was awake too, thinking of Chloe.

Was a coma like being asleep? Did you know if it was night or day? Was Chloe's mind working, even now, calling out to them, searching for a way back through the tangled forest of dreams and memories?

Tormented, he rolled over.

All he had to do was stay here, get undressed, go to sleep. They were drawing him in, these people, and he didn't want to be drawn. He was the artist, he did the drawing. The pun pleased his tired mind; he smiled.

When he woke, the alarm clock in his drawer was pinging.

He groped for it, flicked it off, then looked at the dial blearily.

Midnight.

He'd barely slept an hour. Slowly, he sat up. Had he set the clock? He didn't remember. After a moment he crossed to the open window and edged back the curtain. The drive was dark, but he could make out the outline of a car parked in the lane. It flashed its lights rapidly, a silent glimmer.

Vetch was that sure of him.

It made him want to go straight back to bed, but he didn't, and wearily he came to know that he wouldn't. There was something here he had to find, to touch and understand. He checked his pocket for the key, pulled a dark jacket on and went out onto the landing.

The house was silent.

A clock ticked somewhere. Through an open window the smell of roses drifted.

His parents' door was closed; Chloe's ajar, and the doorway was black. He went quietly down the stairs, let himself out and slipped into the shrubs that lined the drive, so that if his mother looked out the window she wouldn't see him.

The bushes were holly and rhododendron, old and straggly, their centers grown open. Pushing through them, he felt as if he had stepped into that tangle of dreams and branches, the sharp smells of soil and prickly leaf close against his face. And then there was empty space, and the gate. As he unlatched it, it creaked.

The car door opened; Rosa whispered, "Jump in. He's meeting us there."

As they drove he was silent. She gave him one look, then concentrated on the dark lanes, the sharp bends. He wanted to talk to her, but some stubbornness kept him morose. Instead he watched the black humps and hollows of the prehistoric landscape, the immensity of the stones as the car purred past them through the sleeping village.

They parked away from the site, then walked quietly. Two fields on, a fox ran across in front of them. Rosa smiled. "That might be Vetch."

Rob said, "You don't really believe he can shape-shift."

She shrugged. "I have no idea what he can do. To be born from the Cauldron means to have knowledge of the stars and trees and beasts, and to be a bard means entering into the lives of those beings."

"New Age twaddle," he said, wishing Dan was there.

She laughed. "Listen, Rob. The first night he came, he told us a story. His story. About a boy who was once asked to stir a magic Cauldron, full of power, full of inspiration. He stirred it for a year and a day and at the end of that time three hot splashes came out of the Cauldron and burned his hand. He put his hand to his mouth and he tasted them. In that instant he became a poet, the greatest of poets. Taliesin himself. But the woman who owned the Cauldron is the Muse, the Goddess. She hated him for stealing her magic. She hunted him through field and sky and river, each of them changing shape. She still hunts him. She'll kill him if she catches him."

They all spoke this mystical mixed-up language. But the woman had been real. He had no idea what to make of any of it.

"I suppose she's called Clare," he said acidly.

Rosa looked at him in surprise. "In the story she's called Ceridwen."

Rob shook his head. He didn't answer.

Vetch was waiting in the field corner, where the hedges rose up, dark and rustling.

"They'll hear us," Rob said simply.

"They'll neither hear nor see us," Vetch said, "because I'll close their eyes and ears. We'll just be shadows."

"Sure. And the dog?"

"Animals like me. Don't worry, Rob." He held out his hand. After a second, Rob took the key out and dropped it in the man's palm. Vetch smiled.

They climbed the field gate cautiously, its wooden bars slippery with dew, ridged and powdery under Rob's tight grip. On the left, in the darkness of the overgrown hedge, the trailer was a pale glimmer, its windows black squares.

Vetch looked at it. "Two men. Asleep."

"So you've already checked them out."

"If you say so."

Rosa said, "What about the dog?"

"Out here somewhere. Close."

In the darkness, quite unexpectedly, rain began to fall, a soft rain that pattered in the leaves. Vetch ignored it. He walked across the field, sidestepping hollows and mounds of spoil, upturned wheelbarrows, areas cordoned off with fluttering tape and tiny flags. Before him the metal fence loomed up in the dark. The others followed, Rosa close, Rob trailing behind, irritable with guilt.

Vetch reached the fence and took out the key. He slipped it into the lock, but before he could turn it Rosa hissed, "Master!"

A low growl.

The Alsatian had risen up from the grass, lips drawn back, teeth bared, and slavering. The growl was a terrifying threat in its throat, a threat that in seconds would leap and bark and tear and bite.

Rob moved, but Vetch put a hand out to stop him. Then the dark-haired man crouched. He and the dog faced each other.

"Come to me," Vetch commanded.

His voice was quiet, grave. To Rob's surprise the dog's growl ended instantly. It stood, trotted forward, licked Vetch's hand and lay down.

Vetch gave Rob a glance and turned back to the fence.

"Knowledge of beasts," Rosa whispered. "See?"

"Lots of people can do that." But it amazed him, the animal's complete trust. Max was fierce with anyone; even with Jimmy around, Rob had never gone very near him.

The gate opened; Vetch slid in, the others behind him like shadows. Once inside, Rosa clicked on a flaslight.

Droplets of spray hissed through the light like a golden curtain.

Rob watched the two of them as they looked down at the

henge. Rosa stared at the ring of timbers, dark and ominous, rising out of the ridged soil.

She let out a breath of awe. "It's *amazing*. What is it?"

"Clare says an enclosure." Rob was watching Vetch. "A ritual site."

The poet had not moved. He was very still, the light catching his eyes, the glittering spray pattering around him. He stood with his arms around himself, a dark figure against the darkness, and there was a tension about him that made them both fall silent. Now, without speaking, he made his way around the timber ring to the entrance, the narrow gap that Marcus had spent all day troweling. Climbing through, he went to the center of the henge, knelt and, to their astonishment, turned his head and crouched so low that his ear was pressed to the ground. His hands spread on the surface, feeling it gently, as if it was softest fleece. "Have they found anything here?"

"Not as far as I know."

"They will." He raised his head. "I hear the voices of the trees, calling me back. The Trees of the Summer Country, of the Region of the Summer Stars. I hear the birch and the oak, the elm. The forests of the Unworld." He gazed down, propped on his hands, as if the peaty soil was the opening of a well, a transparent glass floor he could stare through. For a moment he seemed lost in that vision. Then, a little stiffly, he climbed to his feet, brushing soil from his fingers. "The way down will be here."

"Down?"

Vetch turned his head. In the darkness, rain glinted,

caught in the hooded glow of the flashlight. Vast shadows flashed and slid over the dark timbers. Concerned, they saw he looked worn and tired. He caught hold of the henge with one hand to support himself, and the fine mist of the sprays that kept it wet fell on him in the torchlight like a million minute stars.

"I told you," he breathed. "The way to Chloe."

Suddenly Rob's patience snapped. Not caring if anyone heard, he yelled, "I should never have brought you here! Get out!"

Rosa said, "Rob—"

"Look at him! Using me! Getting at me through Chloe. It's sick—*I'm* sick for sticking around with you." He was shaking; he clenched his hands.

Vetch straightened and came up to him. "We can help Chloe."

"You can't. No one can."

"You and I can. There is a way to find her."

"Shut up. *Shut up!*" He turned, groping for the gate, blind.

Vetch moved gently around, into his way. "You want her to die, is that it?"

Rob's head whipped up. *"What!"*

"You want her to die. That would end it tidily. It would be over."

"You pathetic—"

"Your parents would mourn, but even for them it would be a secret relief. They would be free to remember Chloe as she was. After a while, all their attention, all their love, would come back to you. It would be just you, and them."

Rob's fist swung in a blow of fury, but before it slammed home Vetch had gripped his wrist. His grasp was surprisingly strong. He said, "It's hard to hear it said aloud. But there is a place inside you that feels these things."

"*No.*"

"It's there, Rob. Dark as coal, a ring around your heart, like this henge. But maybe inside that, deeper and darker, is something else, and it would emerge if you let it, if you scraped at it and dug away at it, let all the creatures of your imagination come out of it, birds and beasts from depths you have no knowledge of. That's where Chloe is, Rob."

Water spray hissed in the silence. Bats flitted over the trees. By the gate Max made a small snuffle as he laid his chin on his paws. Rosa stood watching, her eyes wide and scared.

Slowly, Rob pulled his arm away.

He felt shaken, exhausted. As if some barrier had been scrambled over, some resistance broken down in him. "All right." He looked up. "Find her then. Show me what to do. I'll do whatever you say."

Vetch said, "What we do is wait until the henge is fully exposed. In the meantime, you take me to see her."

Rob stared. "In the nursing home?"

"We can go secretly. Your parents needn't know."

Rob shook his head. He felt bewildered. The bats dizzied him, swooping after invisible insects. "The nurses will tell them."

Vetch smiled his rueful smile. "Say I'm a friend."

"Can you . . . ?" He hated to ask it, loathed himself, had to get it out. "Do you mean you can wake her?"

"I don't know. It depends how many caers she's entered, how far in she is. I will certainly try." He jerked his head at Rosa, and the girl clicked the flashlight off quietly.

And Rob stared, because there was light in the henge, and it was seeping from the ground, the faintest phosphorescence, like trapped starlight. And the bats were pouring from a cavern where the soil had collapsed, tens and hundreds of bats, a whirling cloud of darkness that flapped and twisted and split above the treetops into blurs and zigzags. Their high squeaks punctured the night.

Vetch stood in the curtain of spray, and looked up at them. "Let them fly, Rob," he said.

C. COLL: HAZEL

In the attic room, he dragged furniture across the door. The window shutters creaked, despite the bar across them. Branches slithered. The stairwell must already have been choked.

"They're coming!" I screamed. A tendril of ivy slid under the door; he stamped on it, tore it up. Another came, and another.

I backed against the window. Putting my hands behind me, I fumbled for the shutter catch. If I could open it I could scream for help. To Mum and Dad. To Mac, because surely Mac would hear.

Before I'd found the catch, the ivy was around his wrists and ankles; he yelled, kicking and twisting.

Gently, I unlatched the shutter.

It burst wide.

ter, so after-lunch drinks were in the summerhouse,
blue wooden pavilion under the cedar tree. Rob sat
bench and arranged the painting on the easel, then
ed paint off the palette.

as supposed to be sitting for his portrait; Rob had
ng on it for months, but his enthusiasm came and
y, though, he wanted to lose himself in color. He'd
ace easily enough, but the more he looked the more
reds and even blues there were deep in the mottled
cinated him, filled him with despair.

never finish that," his father muttered.

t to. It's for the portfolio."

t, took out a cigarette and lit it. "Don't paint this in,

u have to? It changes all the shadows."
"

nother stood. "I'll give Maria a hand with clear-

do no such thing, Kate Mcguire. This husband of
do that. You'll have a lie down. You're too pale,

u're a bully, Mac. You talk as if I was still a little
d."

always be a little girl to me."
She went out, walking fast across the lawn, head
st the fine summer rain, and Rob's dad went

oked thoughtfully. "She sleeps all right?"
know."

Chief bard am I among the bards of Elphin,
My country the region of the summer stars.
∞ THE BOOK OF TALIESIN

On Sunday there was mass, and then lunch. Father Mac
always came because Maria did the best roast in
Wiltshire, and afterward he and Rob sometimes walked out on
the downs or along the Ridgeway. Rob didn't want that today.
He realized he didn't really want to be alone with Mac at all,
because his godfather was a man who knew him too well, could
read his moods. Mac already knew something was wrong.

Loitering about at the back of church, he helped an old
man collect hymn books and watched his mother chatting to
her friends at the door. As always she was perfect, her hair
glossy, her makeup professionally expert. Looking at her, he

saw how she animated each sentence, bore the weekly sympathy, the brittle pretense that they were coping, she was coping. He couldn't do that. Maybe people guessed, because none of them ever said anything about Chloe to him.

Dad was outside, in the car. He couldn't do the chatting either.

Mac came down the side aisle in black shirt and trousers and old sandals that flapped. He whipped a pile of newspapers into a bin, growled a few gruff reminders to various parishioners, and said, "Let's go."

As they turned, Rob saw Vetch.

The poet was standing under the statue of Saint Francis, looking up at the kindly wooden face. Saint Francis had birds on his shoulders, tiny wooden sparrows that Rob had always liked ever since he was a kid, when he had daydreamed during long dull sermons that they came alive and flew around the church.

Vetch looked over. Their eyes met.

Rob went tense.

Let them fly, Vetch had said last night, in the cascade of bats. Now, in an instant of crystal clarity Rob knew that he—*he, Rob*—could do that, that he could make the birds come alive and rise from the saint's shoulders if he wanted to, if he could gather up all the power that was in him. If he had faith the size of a mustard seed.

"Who's he?" Mac was behind him, a warm bulk.

Rob blinked. Then he said, "The one I told you about. The druid."

Father Mac was still a moment. Then he crossed to where Vetch was inserting a lighted candle into a holder. The poet's

fingers were thin and delicat
his face.

"Good to see a stranger i
Vetch's calm eyes lifted.
"Really?"

"Many times. Over the c
Mac nodded. His big f
ever threw him. "There mu
here then."

Vetch glanced at Rob.
power, a landscape rayed wit
back at Mac, and they were
the priest's thick bulk. "But

Rob was surprised at M
you tomorrow, Rob," smile
through the main wooden do

"Thought you said
thoughtfully.

"I don't know what he is

"What's this about tomo
abrupt; this time it annoyed

"Nothing. I promised I'd

"A centuries-old wande
around here." Mac turned.
the harmless nutcase I wa
oddly somber, but just then

"Ready?"

"For food, anytime," Ma

It rained l
a decaying
astride the
scraped d

Mac
been wor
went. Too
drawn the
greens an
flesh. It f

"You
"I've
Mac
mind."

"Do y
"Tou
Rob'
ing up."

"You
yours wi
girl."

"And
girl in Ir

"You
"Idio
down ag
after her

Mac
"I do

Chief bard am I among the bards of Elphin,
My country the region of the summer stars.

∞ THE BOOK OF TALIESIN

On Sunday there was mass, and then lunch. Father Mac always came because Maria did the best roast in Wiltshire, and afterward he and Rob sometimes walked out on the downs or along the Ridgeway. Rob didn't want that today. He realized he didn't really want to be alone with Mac at all, because his godfather was a man who knew him too well, could read his moods. Mac already knew something was wrong.

Loitering about at the back of church, he helped an old man collect hymn books and watched his mother chatting to her friends at the door. As always she was perfect, her hair glossy, her makeup professionally expert. Looking at her, he saw how she animated each sentence, bore the weekly sympathy, the brittle pretense that they were coping, she was coping. He couldn't do that. Maybe people guessed, because none of them ever said anything about Chloe to him.

Dad was outside, in the car. He couldn't do the chatting either.

Mac came down the side aisle in black shirt and trousers and old sandals that flapped. He whipped a pile of newspapers into a bin, growled a few gruff reminders to various parishioners, and said, "Let's go."

As they turned, Rob saw Vetch.

The poet was standing under the statue of Saint Francis, looking up at the kindly wooden face. Saint Francis had birds on his shoulders, tiny wooden sparrows that Rob had always liked ever since he was a kid, when he had daydreamed during long dull sermons that they came alive and flew around the church.

Vetch looked over. Their eyes met.

Rob went tense.

Let them fly, Vetch had said last night, in the cascade of bats. Now, in an instant of crystal clarity Rob knew that he—*he*, *Rob*—could do that, that he could make the birds come alive and rise from the saint's shoulders if he wanted to, if he could gather up all the power that was in him. If he had faith the size of a mustard seed.

"Who's he?" Mac was behind him, a warm bulk.

Rob blinked. Then he said, "The one I told you about. The druid."

Father Mac was still a moment. Then he crossed to where Vetch was inserting a lighted candle into a holder. The poet's fingers were thin and delicate; the flame guttered, shadowing his face.

"Good to see a stranger in church."

Vetch's calm eyes lifted. "I've been here before."

"Really?"

"Many times. Over the centuries."

Mac nodded. His big face was expressionless. Nothing ever threw him. "There must be something that attracts you here then."

Vetch glanced at Rob. "Avebury is a hub of spiritual power, a landscape rayed with dreams and visions." He looked back at Mac, and they were eye to eye, the poet thin and dark, the priest's thick bulk. "But of course you know that, Father."

Rob was surprised at Mac's slow nod. Vetch said, "See you tomorrow, Rob," smiled, crossed himself, and went out through the main wooden door.

"Thought you said he was a pagan," Mac said thoughtfully.

"I don't know what he is."

"What's this about tomorrow?" His godfather was always abrupt; this time it annoyed Rob.

"Nothing. I promised I'd take him somewhere."

"A centuries-old wanderer should know all the places around here." Mac turned. "Stay clear of him, Rob. He's not the harmless nutcase I was expecting." His voice sounded oddly somber, but just then Katie came over.

"Ready?"

"For food, anytime," Mac growled.

∞

It rained later, so after-lunch drinks were in the summerhouse, a decaying blue wooden pavilion under the cedar tree. Rob sat astride the bench and arranged the painting on the easel, then scraped dried paint off the palette.

Mac was supposed to be sitting for his portrait; Rob had been working on it for months, but his enthusiasm came and went. Today, though, he wanted to lose himself in color. He'd drawn the face easily enough, but the more he looked the more greens and reds and even blues there were deep in the mottled flesh. It fascinated him, filled him with despair.

"You'll never finish that," his father muttered.

"I've got to. It's for the portfolio."

Mac sat, took out a cigarette and lit it. "Don't paint this in, mind."

"Do you have to? It changes all the shadows."

"Tough."

Rob's mother stood. "I'll give Maria a hand with clearing up."

"You'll do no such thing, Kate Mcguire. This husband of yours will do that. You'll have a lie down. You're too pale, girl."

"And you're a bully, Mac. You talk as if I was still a little girl in Ireland."

"You'll always be a little girl to me."

"Idiot." She went out, walking fast across the lawn, head down against the fine summer rain, and Rob's dad went after her.

Mac smoked thoughtfully. "She sleeps all right?"

"I don't know."

He painted in silence. Rain fell heavily on the glass roof, spattering hard, sheeting in cascades down the gutters and gurgling in drainpipes. The sky darkened; Rob muttered, "Typical," and mixed a little more viridian into the color for the lines between Mac's nose and mouth. The mouth moved.

"They've got money troubles, Rob."

Rob looked up. "No way!"

"How much do you think full-time nursing care costs? Your mother's turned down work. A film, she said."

"She told you?"

A cloud of cigarette smoke. Through it Mac said, "In confidence. But you should know. This job of yours—save the cash. Don't ask them for anything."

The rain crashed. Rob muttered, "I wish you'd shave. Stubble is a nightmare."

He was stunned. They'd always had money. More than enough. His mother was well known, she'd won a BAFTA, her agent was always on the phone with offers. He worked red into blue, lightened it, darkened it.

Money defined him. Dan was always broke, his mother a single parent. Rob paid for everything—it was never an issue. Well, not for him. Maybe Dan resented it. He'd never noticed.

Putting the paint on carefully, he said, "They won't stop paying for Chloe."

"Of course not. But it's ruining them. The longer it goes on."

His hands were shaking. He couldn't do this now: he put the brush down with a clatter that made Mac look over, and then he sat down on the faded blue bench as if the strength had all gone out of him. He knew what this was. It happened when he let himself realize that Chloe was lying there, little Chloe, never moving, never speaking. Right now. *Right now.*

Mac said, "Okay?"

"Great. Just great."

The rain came down harder. Mac got up and stood looking out. Then he gave his harsh laugh. "Just when you thought things couldn't get any worse, here's Dan."

Dan was on the bike. He was going up to the house, but at Rob's shout he came wobbling toward them over the grass, dumped the machine against the streaming glass and stumbled in, soaked to the skin.

Mac ground out his cigarette stub on the step. "Ever heard of a coat?"

"Coats are for wimps." Dan sat, oozing water. "Anyway, it just came up over Waden and caught me. It was dry when I set out." He squeezed out his hair, which he was growing long, because any heavy metal guitarist was nothing without long hair. "Brought you this."

It was a Sunday paper, a tabloid. Rob's dad wouldn't have it in the house.

"A rag," Mac said sourly.

"Yes, but look." Dan folded the paper to an inside page and pointed. The headline was small but lurid. It screamed, SECRET SACRIFICIAL SITE UNCOVERED: WHAT WILD AND WEIRD RITES WENT ON IN DEEPEST WILTSHIRE?

"Oh God," Rob said.

The photographer must have been standing in the lane. Maybe Max had kept him out. But you could see the top of the hedge, and across the field the high metal fence.

Behind this enigmatic structure lies British archaeology's newest and best-kept secret. Older than the pyramids, in the heart of mystic Avebury the black timbers of a lost prehistoric monument are being uncovered in strictest secrecy.

"Where did they get it?" He thought of Clare. She would be so furious!

Dan rolled his eyes. "This is Avebury. People out all hours looking for crop circles, UFOs, little green men. It was bound to get around."

"This is where you're working?" Mac studied the article with distaste. "Why the fixation with human sacrifice? Don't they think our ancestors had other things to do?"

"I'll be the next one," Rob muttered. "She'll think it was me."

"That's hardly reasonable."

He laughed, mirthless. "She's not the reasonable type."

"But it wasn't you. Was it?"

Rob glanced up. His godfather's blue eyes were watching him.

"No," he said quietly. "It wasn't."

Next morning a security guard was at the end of the lane with a cell phone. He checked with someone on the other end before letting Rob through. Wheeling the bike, Rob wondered if it was legal to stop people. After all, this was a right of way.

The field was unrecognizable. A perimeter fence was going up, and the old wooden gate he and Vetch and Rosa had climbed over two nights ago was already replaced with a high metal one. Marcus came out of the trailer, and said, "I really hope you had nothing to do with this."

"Don't be stupid. I wouldn't come back if I had. Don't you think all the security is a bit over the top? Or is Clare spitting nails?"

Marcus's eyes flickered, too late. He walked off.

"I warned you, Rob." Clare was standing behind him. Her cold glare chilled him. "I'm surprised you dare show your face."

"It wasn't me!"

"Who then? The dog?"

"Anyone. The farmer could have gossiped in the pub. National Trust people, your students, anyone. It's not fair to blame me, but if you want me to go, I'll go." And stuff your job, he thought, turning, skewing the bike in the mud, hot and angry. Guilty.

Her voice stopped him dead. "This Vetch. Does he have a small scar on his forehead? Does he have three burns on the back of his hand?"

After a moment he said, "Yes."

She swore.

The key. He had to get the key back.

He turned to face her.

She looked tired and fed up. "You told him?"

"No, I didn't. He knew already. Honestly."

To his surprise she laughed, a harsh amusement. "Oh, I believe you. And no doubt he's found a few new devotees. Women probably. Hanging on every word he says."

Rob rubbed the handlebar of the bike. "Was that what you used to do?"

He thought she'd be furious. Instead she said, "Oh yes. I was a student, Rob, in my last year at uni. And I was the best in my year, a highflier, expected to get a first. Everyone expected me to be anything I wanted."

She sat on an upturned bucket, glanced around to see where Jimmy was, then lowered her voice. "I met . . . Vetch in Oxford. His name was Gwion then. He wasn't a student, or a tutor, but he did occasional things for the Department of Celtic . . . readings, talks on Welsh poetry. That was his thing. We . . . got to be friends."

Rob found it hard to imagine. She must have been a lot less hard.

"Looking back, he was fascinating. He talked about poetry, about how the Celtic myths might go right back to pre-historic times, that the stories in them, of goddesses, and battles with trees and glass castles, were legends told by people who built the henges. Bronze Age. Maybe even Neolithic." She laughed, sour. "I thought he was right. I neglected my studies. I read myths, wrote essays that my tutors despaired of, full of theories, the more unlikely the better. . . . I wore crazy dresses and went to festivals, lived in squalor. And yes, got into drugs, though Vetch never was. But I had to keep up with him. He lived in a dreamworld of ideas and stories. All I wanted was his respect. And then one day he vanished. Just upped and left. I was devastated. I suppose it was a miracle I even took the exams in the end."

She was silent so long he said, "You failed?"

"I got a third. A third! I could forget trying to get a research post. I was a third-rate archaeologist with no job, no credibility and nowhere to live." She tugged her braid out, and tied it up again quickly, her fingers working nervously. "It's taken me years to work my way back up, and no one is going to ruin it. Especially *him*." As if she was embarrassed, had said too much, she stood quickly. "However it happened, the news is out, I can't stop it. And we need you, Rob. Now more than ever. We have to work at top speed; every bloody pressure group, coven, and chapter will be here in hours. We have to get the henge timbers out of the ground. Once that's done they can hold all the press conferences they want. It will be too late."

The idea of the henge being uprooted terrified him. But he just nodded and went to lock up the bike.

The hole the bats had streamed out of was gone; Jimmy had troweled it away. Rob didn't ask about it. They worked ferociously all morning. The rattle and crash of the fence builders shattered the quiet of the site, but behind that were other new noises: voices in the lane, cars, the trill of Clare's cell phone. Once, when she was sitting on the bank arguing into it fiercely, Rob walked out of the inner fence toward the portable toilet, but at the last minute slid into the office and got the key into the back of the drawer in seconds. It would take more than a key to get in here now. It would take a parachute.

Someone else had the same idea. At about eleven a helicopter came over, cruising low.

Clare swore in fury. "My God, these people have got a nerve."

Someone was leaning out of it with a camera.

"TV?" Rob muttered.

"Probably. I refused them access. They'll have a good view of the henge from up there though."

Darkhenge was alive. That was how it seemed to him. Hour by hour the timbers were growing, soaring up out of the churned peat. By midmorning they were as tall as he was, and if you were outside you could no longer see in. Solid and glistening under its mist of water, the wooden henge stood erect, the ancient knot-holes and gnarled scars where branches had been lopped still seamed with hatchet marks. Crouched, troweling, his arms and back aching, Rob sliced the fudgelike mud, his eyes attuned to the faintest differences in color, knowing already the sludgy smears of clay, the knobbliness of mud-coated flint nodules, the stench of leeched worms. His overalls were saturated, the knees so clotted with wet soil he could feel it on the inside. He knelt in it, and his fingers were ingrained with earth in every crack of his skin and under his nails, so that he no longer recognized them as his. There was nothing to do but dig. The world outside had faded away. Here, in the clogged wet warmth of the henge, there was only the uncovering, a feverish, obsessive desire.

They snatched a few muddy sandwiches at about noon, and Jimmy brought mugs of tea out. Drinking it, Rob felt himself come back from somewhere; when Clare and Marcus spoke he had to listen hard to understand the words, as if their sounds held meanings only slowly recognized.

Was this how it felt to come out of a coma? To awake, months, years, centuries later? He frowned, tipping the last drips of tea onto the mud like an offering. It wasn't like him to think like that. Archaeology gave you too much time to think.

By three o'clock the henge timbers were higher than his head. All afternoon the muggy heat thickened, the sky grew overcast and heavy, zigzagged with midges and flying ants.

His skin crawled and prickled with heat rash and itches. Surely the prehistoric ground level must be close now. Thinking of what Vetch had said, he glanced at Marcus, who was dreamily scraping in the center. "Found anything there?"

The man looked up, startled. "No. Clean as a whistle."

"What might there be?"

Marcus shrugged, and Jimmy stabbed his trowel in the soil and stood, stretching, as if the words had broken a spell. "Possibly a foundation burial. It's usually a child, or young woman. Or there may just be a deposit, some antler, those weird chalk balls."

A rustle disturbed him. Birds fluttered down, small birds. Jackdaws. They were coming from the trees in the next field, a flock, swooping, and as Rob turned his head he saw that they were landing on the henge timbers, a pecking, flapping circle, rising and settling, never still. The men watched, amazed, in a ring of birds. Marcus jumped up, but the jackdaws didn't take fright, not until Clare clanged the metal gate and came up to the henge, and at that moment the whole flock rose into the air like a cloud, circling, chattering, screeching.

Then they flew away.

"God," Jimmy said. "This place is weird."

Close, toward the downs, thunder rumbled.

"We're going to have to stop." Clare's face was set, her blond hair streaked with mud. She shook her head irritably. "Everyone's on the phone. The Trust, English Heritage, the papers, my head of department. They all want in. Our cover's blown."

She sat, disconsolate, on the wet soil. "If I ever find out who leaked this—"

"Will they sack you?" Rob asked quickly.

"I don't think so. But it won't be my baby now." Thunder rumbled again; she looked up. "Weather's closing in anyway. We'll shut down for today. There'll be full security here overnight."

Jimmy whistled. "Expensive."

Marcus picked up his trowel, crouched, looked carefully, scraped with it.

They all watched him. His body had suddenly become intent. Even Rob recognized it.

"What?" Clare hissed.

"Not sure. Looks like the central deposit."

"Oh bloody hell! What a time to find it."

They knelt beside him. He scraped twice. Mud unpeeled like the pith of an orange.

Under it, a snake of wood curved into the soil.

"A carving?" Rob asked, astonished. Whatever he had expected, it wasn't this.

The trowel opened another. And another. A tangle of wooden writhing, black ridges.

"Branches," Marcus muttered, cutting quickly.

"No." Clare had her face close to it, her fair hair falling onto the buried mystery. "Not branches. A tree, yes, but not branches. Roots."

"Roots? But you mean..."

She looked at them, her face white in a crack of lightning. Her answer was a whisper, almost drowned by the roar of thunder. *"A tree. Upside down."*

Q. QUERT: APPLE

The trees were so angry; their anger was terrible. It was mine and it was all toward him. When he turned I was already half out—he yelled and grabbed me around the waist, hauled me back, and I screeched and kicked. Powdery lichened branches held me; my hands slid along them; nuts and leaves snapped and cut me. I dug my nails in. I saw willows, blackthorn, oak reaching out to rescue me.

"Help me!" I screamed. "Mac! Can you hear me?"

The trees had my hands. They pulled me through the window.

*I was the designer
who built Nimrod's tower.
I spent three lifetimes
In the dungeons of Arianrhod.*

∞ THE BOOK OF TALIESIN

"I could come with you."

"It's fine. It's fine. I told you." Running into Dan outside the pub just at this moment was a nightmare. Squeezed into the porch out of the pelting rain, Rob moved aside to let a group of tourists by. "I'm . . . Someone's giving me a lift."

"But you usually only go on Fridays." Dan folded his arms, looking past Rob at the suddenly crowded bar. "There's nothing wrong, is there? There's no change?"

"No change." Rosa's car would arrive any second. "Go back to your illegal pint."

"Oh, I get it. It's a girl! Who is she? Come on!"

"Not . . . not a girl."

It was too late. The blue car pulled up by the drenched picnic tables and the door opened. Rosa waved. Vetch said, "Ready?"

Rob nodded. Then he mumbled, "This is Dan. This is Vetch. And Rosa," and got in without looking at Dan, without even hearing him say anything, though he felt his disbelief as if it was a stinging radiation in the air.

Then they were driving, out of the ring of the great stones, through the gap in the green bank, steady, toward Swindon.

"A friend?" Vetch asked quietly.

"The best." He turned, glaring at the man in the front seat. "Was it you who told the papers?"

"Of course not." Vetch's calm eyes held his steadily. "You know very well it's the last thing I want. Everyone will be crawling over the site. The security will already have been increased. That's so, isn't it?"

Rob's lips were pressed tight. He didn't want to believe him, but he did. He breathed out and said, "New fence. Guards everywhere. She's livid."

"She. That will be Clare."

Rob remembered. "She's seen you. She blames you."

Vetch turned to gaze out through the rain-streaked glass at the green blurs of the downs. "I knew she would," he murmured. "Her anger with me is as deep as the forest."

Into the silence Rob said, "There's a tree in the center. An upturned tree."

Rosa swerved the car. *"What?"*

Vetch didn't flicker. "Of course there is."

In the mirror Rosa's eyes met Rob's. She looked astonished.

"How do you know?" Rob snapped, rebellious. "You couldn't know."

Vetch closed his eyes. He didn't answer.

At the nursing home Rosa pulled into the parking lot and turned the engine off. "I can come back if—"

"No need. We'll find our own way home." Vetch sat up and smiled at her. "Have a good evening."

Outside, he watched the car drive off.

Then he turned and looked at Rob through the rain. "I'll try my best, Rob," he said quietly, "but as things are, I don't know how much I can do. Don't get your hopes up."

"I haven't got any hopes."

Vetch was silent. Then he nodded, and turned toward the lighted entrance.

Sister Mary was in the hall. She was surprised, Rob knew, but she covered it well. "Rob! We weren't expecting anyone tonight. Your mum phoned earlier—"

"I told her I'd come instead." He said it quickly, because it was a lie. "The filming's taken longer than they thought."

Sister Mary said, "Such an exciting sort of life!" But she was looking at Vetch.

"Can we go in?" Rob said.

"Oh yes. She's had her hair washed today. Such lovely hair."

In the lift Rob said, "She gushes."

"She has great compassion." Vetch folded his arms, as if he was nervous. "I could feel it. She was also a little doubtful of me."

"She hasn't seen you before." Rob was nervous too, feeling the dread that always invaded him in this lift, as if it was a shadow that lived here, waiting to enter him, because it left him here too, on the way out. Fear of going in. Of seeing her.

The room was dark, with one lamp lit. Outside the open window the rain had stopped, so that only a line of drops dripped from the swiveled pane.

Vetch went up to the bed and looked down at Chloe. "She looks very much like you," he murmured.

Rob shrugged. Chloe's hair was fine and fair; it shone, and he could smell the faint clean smell of shampoo, the one she always used. She wore new blue pajamas he hadn't seen before. Vetch pulled the chair closer and sat. He picked up Chloe's hand, his delicate fingers as white as hers.

Rob bit his lip. "Do you have to do that?"

"It helps. But if you—"

"No. It doesn't matter."

And yet if she was aware somewhere, she'd be furious. So he said aloud, "This is Vetch, Chloe. He's . . . all right."

"High praise." Vetch put Chloe's fingers down on the white sheet and rubbed the back of his hand over his mouth. "This room makes it difficult. All these machines . . ."

"For God's sake! We can hardly turn them off!" Rob suddenly had no idea why he'd come. Why either of them had come.

Vetch nodded. "No." Then he said, "I suppose I just hate hospitals." He reached into his coat and pulled out the small bag.

"What is that?"

"The crane-skin bag. It contains words. All a poet needs."

He opened the drawstring neck and tipped out some small sticks onto the bed. Rob came closer.

The shaven twigs were about three inches long, and looked

like hazel, because some of the bark was still on the back of them. Each had one side sliced smooth, and into its edge were cut a series of stiff, angular lines. Some horizontal, others leaning.

"What are they?"

Vetch glanced up. "Letters. The alphabet is an ancient one, called ogham."

The room had dimmed. Now Vetch moved the pile of Mum's red knitting, switched off the lamp, and it seemed black. "Open the window," he said. "And stay over there. Don't come closer until I tell you."

Rob hesitated, then did it. When he turned there was a new sound in the room. It lay behind the quiet regular beeps of the monitors, behind the sound of the breeze in the trees outside. It was a whisper, a murmur of words.

He leaned back against the windowsill, sweating. Anxiety was tight in his chest; he was breathing too hard, and yet there seemed to be no air. Something was sucking the air out of the room.

It was the words. They were in no language he knew, and there were so many of them. Small shadows fluttered and crackled and landed on the bed—moths, he thought, or maybe not, maybe letters, the stiff letters coming alive, crawling, unfurling, flying. And yet there were real moths in here too, blundering through the open window, their shadows distorted as they banged against the lit glass panel over the door.

Vetch leaned forward. He touched Chloe's forehead, her closed eyelids, her mouth. His fingers were thin and damp, and Rob felt that touch and shivered. But Chloe didn't move.

Vetch said, "There are many ways into the Unworld. A

door opens, a bird sings. Someone invites you, someone takes your hand. You go in, you listen. It only seems like seconds. Out here, lifetimes pass." He had glanced around the room; now he lifted the vase of flowers and took the circular woven placemat from underneath. He placed the mat on the bed, took one of the small sticks, and pushed the base in, so it stood upright.

Very slightly, the murmur in the air modulated.

"Once you're there, you must not eat or drink. If you do, you may never come out." He looked up. "Do you understand?"

"It's . . . That's old stuff. Legends."

Vetch slotted a second notched twig into the base. "Yes. These days people would say the pathways of her brain have been altered, that some cortex or node has been damaged. Each time cloaks its knowledge in imagery. As the men who built the henges did."

A third twig stood upright. Rob felt the darkness gather; behind him curtains drifted, a soft touch on his arm. Sounds whispered and crisped like wings.

He took a step closer.

"Stay back." Carefully, listening intently, Vetch put in another twig, then another. They had begun to make a tiny wooden circle around the circumference of the placemat, the notched shaven wood close together, the words a rampart.

He was re-creating the henge.

As each new sliver of wood stood upright, the echo and murmur in the room coalesced and strengthened. Syllables began to form, whole phrases in the air, a chanting.

"Who's saying it?" Rob whispered.

Vetch didn't answer. He was concentrating, his fine

fingers adjusting the pegs of the henge, swapping them, turning them, as if it was some musical instrument he tuned, and with each addition and movement the poem—because it was a poem now—seemed nearer, though it was coming from very far away, distorted and scrambled, as if a radio wasn't quite on the station.

Rob was stiff with tension.

"There are seven fortresses in that world." Vetch's voice was strained. "Seven caers, each stronger, deeper inside. She may be too far in for me to reach her. He would take her from castle to castle."

The circle was half formed. The music lost static, became a single voice. Miles and eternities away, it sang.

A bulb in the corridor flickered. Somewhere in the building a window banged. Rob moved instantly, across to the door, but there was no lock. He stood with his back pressed against it. "Hurry," he gasped. "Hurry."

"I can't." Vetch's hands were shaking; sweat gleamed on his forehead. "Can't hurry this."

Three parts of the circle were formed. As the poet's long fingers slid the twigs in, he seemed to be pushing against great pressure, as if the tiny henge resisted formation; then the poem swelled and receded, a burst of nonsensical, delirious words. *"Shining bright star... I fight, I struggle... grass and trees are hastening, hurrying; see them, far traveler, wonder at them, warrior, call upon your god, on the saints of your god..."*

A chant like a spell, beating and rhythmic. Other sounds were wound in it; he realized they were the bleeps and beats of the monitors, Chloe's pulse and heartbeat, forming the syllables.

"Save us from rage ... from the anger of the trees, the onrush of branches, a thousand princes, the hosts of the enemy..."

Vetch pushed the last but one twig in. The circle was black. It sang in electric pulses and a girl's voice, high and clear.

"The enchanted trees, the magic forest, its battle-line comes, we fight it with the music of harps..."

The last sliver. He held it tight, moved it down. It touched.

All the monitors spat.

Rob gasped.

Chloe's eyes flickered.

Instantly all around the room, alarms screamed. A gust of rain billowed the curtains. Rob flung himself forward. "She moved! I saw her move!"

"Help me!" Was it Vetch who said that? There were leaf shadows all over him, on the ceiling, the walls. The wires of the machines were curling like roots.

Rob grabbed the poet's shaking hands. Together they held the sliver steady, brought it back, guided it into place, forced it down. The circle was closed.

Chloe jerked. She gave a great gasp. Outside people were running, shouting; the door burst open.

"Keep them back!" Vetch yelled in fury; grabbing her arms, he dragged her up, off the pillow. "Chloe! Climb out! Climb out to us!"

"Willows," she breathed. *"Blackthorn..."*

The henge slid to the floor, rolled. "I summon you," Vetch commanded. "I call you back! Chloe!"

"Oak ... the King..." Over his shoulder, she looked at Rob.

The light snapped on. "No!" Rob howled, but he was

shoved aside by frantic nurses, a doctor, Sister Mary.

"No! She's waking! He's waking her!"

A great hand held his shoulder like a clamp. "What in God's name is going on here?" Mac whispered furiously behind him.

Vetch was held tight by a security guard. He looked haggard and worn out.

Half off the bed, Chloe lay crumpled, eyes closed, her shining hair a mess.

The doctor turned. "Get out of here," he raged. "Before I have you thrown out! Father, do you know this man?"

Mac glanced at Vetch. Then he growled, "Yes. Calm down. He hasn't hurt her—"

"He could have killed her!"

"She was waking!" Rob was shivering with anger and despair. "She was almost awake . . . she looked at me—"

"Impossible." Hurriedly, the doctor checked Chloe's eyes, her breathing.

"You heard the alarms. . . ."

"The monitors must have been disconnected. I think we should call the police."

"There's no need for that," Mac snapped.

Vetch smiled wearily. "Do what you want," he said, his voice hoarse. Then, as if it was a great effort, he lifted up his left wrist. "But if nothing happened," he whispered, "how do you explain this?"

Chloe's fingers were curled tightly in his.

She was holding his hand.

M. MUIN: VINE

"Why?"

It was all I could stammer out. I was shaking, furious. "I saw Rob! He was there through the trees! Why are you keeping me here!"

He slammed the bar across the shutters. Snapped ends of vines curled on the floor.

"I'm sorry, Chloe," he gasped, "but it's for your own good, believe me. The forest is a terrible thing, relentless. It might destroy us both."

"Rubbish!"

He grabbed my arms. The secret stairway was in the wall; as he pulled me toward it, I shoved him, and he fell against the wall.

I was so angry I screamed. Then I tore off his mask.

O wise druids,
do you prophesy of Arthur?
Or is it me you dream of?
∞ THE BOOK OF TALIESIN

Father Mac came back into his sitting room and stood in front of the empty fireplace. "Want to tell me about it?"

It wasn't a request. Rob was silent. Then he said, "I had no idea he could do anything like that. I thought he just wanted to see her. . . ."

"Your sister is some sort of exhibit now?" It was hard and it hurt, but Rob was too tired and drained to be angry.

"No." He turned. "You saw! She had hold of him. Her eyes were open; she spoke. If they hadn't stopped him . . ."

"She might be awake, yes. Or she might be dead. The sister said the readings had gone through the roof. Heart, blood pressure." Seeing Rob close his eyes, Mac came around and sat on the greasy leather armchair. His voice softened. "Don't worry. She was stable again before we came away. What exactly did he do?"

"Sang." It was the only way Rob could explain, though he knew the words had been more a chant than a song, and Vetch hadn't spoken them. He lifted his head, hopelessly. "And made a circle of pieces of wood, with letters on them. Like the henge."

Mac rasped his stubbly chin. "I told you to stay clear of him. He's not . . . safe."

Rob looked up. "How?"

"I can feel a power in him, though I'm loath to admit it. Something old. Ancient. Whether he means well or not I don't know. I do know that he ought to be in the hospital himself; I've seen more sick men than most, and he's one. Serious, I'd guess."

They were silent a moment. Then Mac leaned back, creaking the chair. "Is he homeless?"

"Not sure. Probably."

"You'd both better stay over. Phone them at home."

When he did, there was only his father there; Rob said he would be staying at Mac's. "Fine, you carry on." His father's voice sounded preoccupied. "No one else is here. Your mother's stuck in London. I'll have Maria's pizza all to myself."

Putting the phone down, Rob stared out at the dim horizon of the downs. The whole family was falling apart. As if Chloe had been some central pin, holding them tight around her, and now there was no center, no focus. As if they weren't strong enough on their own.

When Vetch came downstairs he looked pale, the mark on his forehead more noticeable. His hair was wet, and slicked back, as if he'd splashed water over himself. He sat quietly at a table by the window, still in his dark coat.

"You're both staying here tonight," Father Mac said gruffly.

"Thank you. But—"

"No buts. I'm not driving you back and the buses have finished."

"We could walk." But Vetch smiled as he said it, and added, "I wonder you want me here, Father."

Mac leaned forward. "Tell me about yourself. Explain to me who you are and what you want. This boy is my godson, and more than that, his immortal soul is in my care. I won't let any harm come to him. And no New Age bullshit, please."

Rob stared. Vetch just laughed. He drew in a breath, but Mac held up a hand, went to his sideboard and took out a glass. He poured red wine into it and came back. "Drink that first. You look washed out."

Vetch sipped it. When he spoke his voice was stronger; he looked out at the downs. "What I am or who I am is difficult to explain. I've had many names and lived in many times and places, but my real home is not here. It's in a place I call the Unworld, or Annwn. Another dimension, another reality. A wood of dreams, a landscape of sinew and stone. You might call it the Imagination."

Mac leaned back and spread his feet out. He looked resigned but said nothing.

"I was drawn here now because of the Darkhenge. It

was built about four thousand years ago, by the men and women of this place, in a certain season when the stars were correct and the harvest was in. I watched them build it."

Over the top of the glass his gray eyes met Mac's; the priest stared back, expressionless. "That must have been fascinating."

Vetch smiled. "Oh, it was."

"You didn't help?"

"I sang to them. Sang of the Cauldron, and the trees. When the great oak was stripped of its bark I chanted the poet's secret words."

Mac took out a cigarette. "Go on."

"The henge is a ritual enclosure, something like a church, something like a healing place. Those who have the knowledge and the ability may use it as a gateway. I've been here too long; my existence is thinning, being eaten away. It's time I went home. The henge is my way back."

"And Chloe?"

Vetch sighed. Then he said, "I had hoped I could find her, but she's moving deeper in. She's trapped in there, in herself, her memories, her fears. If I get back, I'll look for her. I can't promise anything though. I think it's possible she's being held against her will."

Mac glanced at the clock as it struck eleven, but he wasn't seeing it. He had that look Rob recognized from painting his portrait, that focused, formidable hardness. "You seem to know a great deal about this."

"Knowledge is my business."

"As a poet."

Vetch gave his quiet smile. "As one of the Cauldron-born, yes."

"A druid."

"Perhaps bard is a better word. Perhaps priest."

Mac scowled. "I should throw you out now."

"I don't think you will, Father. Because time is short. Now the authorities know about the henge they will act quickly; it will be uncovered and probably removed for conservation. Has Rob told you about the central deposit?"

"No."

"It's a tree." Vetch put the glass down and leaned forward. All at once he seemed tense with excitement. "A great oak. It was a holy tree, a shaman's tree, lightning-struck, bone white. It was selected with great care; a whole tribe working on uprooting it for months, at special times and seasons, digging around it, easing it out entire, a vast tangle of roots. Once they had dragged it to the site, they stripped it of bark, trimmed the trunk and inverted it. It has become an axis, a pole linking this place and the Unworld. It leads inside. To the world within."

Mac blew out smoke and glanced at Rob. "Is that so."

He was elaborately sarcastic, but Vetch was watching him carefully. "I see you also know about this."

Mac looked back at him hard. "You may well be eternal. But so am I. So are all of us. And yes, I know there are other worlds. Places outside this reality. We call one of them Hell."

Vetch looked down, fingering the string of the bag that trailed from his pocket. "She's not there," he said softly. "You don't think that."

To Rob's surprise Mac snorted out a laugh. "No," he said. "She's not there."

"Nor do I come from such a place."

Mac stood up, a great upheaval from the leather chair. "No, my son," he said, looking down. "I don't think you do. Judging by the remnants of your accent, I'd say you came from Wales."

By eleven o'clock next morning the tree roots were uncovered.

Pausing a moment in the welter of mud and midge-haunted heat, Rob put a hand out and rubbed the smooth black bole, the hollow center. Already Marcus had begun to speculate: the hollow had held water, or blood, or a sacred object, or a corpse to be picked clean by hawks.

It had been photographed from every angle; Rob had a longing to draw it, to involve himself with that tangle of seamed and smooth wooden threads, but there wasn't time.

Everything had speeded up. For a start, Clare was no longer in charge. A bearded man in battered wellingtons and a blue waterproof coat over his suit was conducting a hurried press conference at the entrance to the metal fence; his name was Warrington and he was from English Heritage. Other new people came and went, talking, photographing, making excited comments. Clare was around; she had spent most of the morning in the trailer being interviewed on the phone, and now he saw her talking volubly at some camera. It seemed she was getting her say in, at least.

When she finished, she hurried over, looking pleased.

"Lab's available for the dendro and the carbon dating,"

she said to Jimmy, over Rob's head. "Take the samples this afternoon."

When she was gone, Rob said, "Dendro...?"

"Chronology. Tree rings. You count them and work out the date the tree was cut."

Rob cleaned a scrape of soil. Another inch of the tree's side emerged into daylight. Perhaps he was the first to see it for thousands of years. Then a thought pierced like a cold sliver into his mind. He looked up. "How?"

"What?"

"How do you count them? The thing's still in the ground..."

"Not for long. But I'll cut a slice out."

Appalled, Rob said, "Cut?"

Jimmy grinned. "With a chain saw, clever boy."

Rob didn't move, chilled with fear. When he looked back down, he barely saw what he was doing.

"She's linked to the henge," Vetch had said that morning on the bus. "The henge is the way to her, and by the ogham twigs I may have made the connection even stronger." He had sounded anxious. Maybe this was what he had feared. It was the only way to Chloe. And if they took a chain saw to it...

Twelve o'clock was the lunch break and it was five to now. Suddenly Rob scraped the trowel clean, dumped it in the bucket and raced for his bike, pushing it past the parked cars and swinging on. Clare came out and yelled after him, "Don't be late! This afternoon is crucial!" He waved back, wobbling off over the white chalk ruts, swerving to avoid a tractor coming around. He rode hard, the wind in his face, the muscles in his calves tight.

A chain saw! He had to find Vetch!

Cutting through the lanes, he turned onto the A4 and struck recklessly across it, almost hit by a truck blaring past. Across the road he whipped into the lane to Avebury.

Whizzing past Falkner's Circle, where Chloe had fallen, he thought briefly again about the girl on the horse he had seen there, and glanced up the track by the hedge, but it was overgrown and silent.

"Be careful!" he hissed aloud. *"Wherever you are, Chloe, be careful!"*

The camp under the beech trees was quiet. Smoke rose from a fire and a little girl played in some mud. The woman he remembered as Megan came out of a tent and stared as the bike slewed over.

"Where's Vetch?" Rob gasped.

"At the Cove. They're waiting for you."

He stared, then turned and ran back inside the vast embankment, clicking open the gate on the right and squeezing into the long grass of the northeast quadrant of the massive Avebury ring. The grass was ankle high and tussocky, chewed by sheep who stared and wandered away from him, unbothered by people. Few stones still stood here, and visitors usually walked along the high bank looking down, the white trails of erosion clear in the chalk.

In the center of a fragmented inner ring an enormous triad of stones had once made an open-sided square, called the Cove. One was gone, fallen centuries ago; the two remaining stones leaned with their heads together, a right angle of mystery.

The Cauldron tribe was there. All of them, with backpacks, flags, banners, kindling, drums. One man held a vast cloud of multicolored balloons with SAVE DARKHENGE printed on them. Dogs barked; a few children ran around with streamers.

Vetch was sitting with his back against the larger Cove stone, looking up onto the Ridgeway. When he saw Rob, he stood.

Breathless, Rob doubled over.

"They've started?" Vetch said.

"This afternoon . . . chain saw . . ." He could barely speak. He could only think of Chloe, lying in bed. So unprotected. "Will it hurt her? This link . . ."

"Don't worry," Vetch said quietly. But his face was white. He looked at Rosa. "Are you ready?"

She pulled a hairgrip open with her teeth and pushed it into her hair. "Ready. Cars are in the lane."

Vetch nodded, then, seeing Rob frown, looked over his shoulder. Dan was jumping the fence from the road. Vetch picked up the crane-skin bag and slipped it in his pocket. "Not much time, Rob."

Rob nodded. As Vetch and Rosa led the tribe through the grass, Dan ran up. "What's going on? What are you *doing* with this crowd?"

"Are you working this afternoon?"

"No. Why?"

"There's going to be some trouble at the dig."

Dan's eyes lit. "Trouble? What sort?"

"Protests . . . I don't know. The henge is important, Dan. Vetch thinks he can wake Chloe, but the henge is part of it; we have to keep it safe and it's under threat. Will you come?" It was blurted out and he knew it sounded unhinged, because of the way Dan was looking at him.

"Chloe? Come on, Rob—"

"I know, I *know*, but he's . . . He can do it."

Dan shrugged, bemused. "I never thought you'd get mixed up with all that crazy stuff. Does Father Mac know?"

"Mac!" Rob grabbed his arm, hauled him toward the lane. "We need him! Have you got your phone?"

After a moment Dan took it out. "Not much left on it."

Rob pushed Mac's number, then, when the priest answered, said quickly, "It's the henge. It's in danger. Can you come?"

Mac hesitated. "I've got someone here. I'll come as soon as I can."

"Do something else for me. In Chloe's room, under the covers, there's a book. Her diary. Bring it with you."

Mac made a grunting noise. "Are you sure?"

"Yes."

"I'll be an hour or so. Stay calm." Then, just before the phone went down, his voice growled, "And keep an eye on that bloody druid."

They piled out of cars and vans, a noisy multicolored crowd surging up the lane. The security guard had barely time to open his mouth before he was firmly pushed into the hedge. The tribe swarmed into the field, onto the trailer, around the metal fence that protected the henge. One or two of them leaped up and pulled at it, tugging and yelling; it shook and Jimmy came running out. He stopped dead; Rob grinned at the dismay on his face.

Easing back into the shadow of the trees, he said, "What about me?"

"We need you on the inside," Rosa said. "Go back to work as usual. Is this chain saw already on site?"

"There are tools in the van. It may be there."

Rosa gave a jerk of her head; two of the tribe raced off.

"And the dog?"

"Don't worry about the dog," Vetch said quietly. He was crouched against the hedge, looking pale. His breathing seemed shallow.

Rosa crouched by him, anxious. "Master, tell us what you want us to do."

His fingers working open the drawstring, Vetch said, "I'm all right, Rosa. I can last out. As soon as the moon rises I can enter the henge, but we have to keep it untouched until then." He tipped out a whorled shell, a beetle that crawled away, a piece of antler, and three white berries that looked like mistletoe. He scooped the berries up and ate them quickly. Pulling a face, as if they were sour, he looked at her. "*Untouched*. That means you have to make as much of a fuss as you can."

"No problem! We've phoned every TV company and conservation group for miles around. Wiltshire Sound, pagans, archaeologists, locals. It'll be the biggest gathering here since the Silbury Hill work gangs packed up."

Vetch smiled, and touched her arm lightly. "Thank you, Rosa."

She blushed. "We'll get you back home, Master. I promise you. You should rest now."

"One more thing." He looked at Rob. "The henge has emerged. It's open. Other things may come through. Be warned."

Rob nodded. He turned, straight into Dan, then pushed past him into the lane.

"Rob." Breathless, Dan caught up and grabbed him. "He's sick, you can see that. On something too, probably. You mustn't . . . None of this has anything to do with Chloe . . ."

"He woke her." Rob turned. "Just for a second. I was there, I saw it. And he can do it again."

"You're . . . It's been so long. You're clutching at straws."

Rob stopped. He looked up and knew his face was stricken and hard. "Yes. All right. Straws, pieces of twig, a timber henge, anything. It's all gone, Dan, all our lives, everything. We're like hollow people, getting up, going to work, eating, sleeping, and none of it's real, it's all pretending, acting. My mother's living out one of her films; my father's directing an invisible play. And all I can do is draw, because that makes sense of the terror; I can tidy it, arrange it on a page. Till Vetch came I hid it all away, inside colors, buried it under layers of paint. But it's like Darkhenge, it's emerging, second by second, and it's huge and all around me and I can't ignore it anymore." His voice almost broke. "I can't!"

Dan was silent. Then he put an awkward hand out. "All right. I'm with you."

Behind, in the field, the drums began to beat.

G. GORT: IVY

I should have guessed.

As we ran down the glass stair and the bubble-seamed tunnel, reflections of ourselves ran beside us, a figure with my lichen-stained hair, and another in the mask he wore under the other; a face made of ivy leaves.

Above, through the transparent roof, I could see all the roots of the forest, an unguessable tangle, a million filaments stretching and reaching down into the soil, from gnarled lumps vast as boulders to threads tinier than worms. The forest drank, and in its depths snakes slid and insects burrowed. Billions of ants scurried like thoughts below it; its millennia of leaves fell and crushed and soaked and rotted.

He stopped so suddenly I banged into him, breathless.

"Listen!"

He caught my arm. Far off, the faintest whine. As if in the forest someone had started up a saw, had begun to cut the trees.

I couldn't answer. Pain was soaking my side. Blood dripped from my arm.

"Chloe!" he gasped.

I have been a roebuck on the hill,
I have been a tree stump...
I have been an axe in the hand.

∞ THE BOOK OF TALIESIN

All afternoon the noise was incredible.

As Rob sat on the wheelbarrow, he saw how Clare prowled inside the metal fence, never coming out, as if she guarded the henge herself.

Her scream of rage when the tribe had burst through the perimeter fence still haunted him. But there was no battle.

It was a standoff.

For hours the tribe had held the field. They lounged in patient groups, occupied the trailer, gave balloons to the press and the three bemused policemen who talked to them gravely. To remove them would have meant force, and evidently that was going to be a last resort.

When the TV cameras came back—more than this morning, Rob saw—the whole thing developed into an interview frenzy, with heated arguments and backings-down and denials.

"Of course," the man called Warrington repeated endlessly to a heckling reporter, "the henge is our first priority. Rumors of the use of a chain saw are totally exaggerated. At most a sliver would be removed...."

Howls of protest drowned him from the tribe. And they weren't alone. As Rosa had said, people were arriving all the time. There were cars and bikes backed up for miles down the lane. Local Women's Institute types turned up with garden chairs and sandwiches. Men who looked like archaeologists and birdwatchers and stalwarts of local history societies were everywhere. Somewhere a radio was playing "The Ride of the Valkyries." Someone said a coven from Swindon was on the way.

"Protest!" Dan muttered. "It's more like a garden fête."

Rob nodded absently. Clare was beckoning him.

He went over, stepping between a line of sprawled Hell's Angels lying across the trampled grass.

"You brought them here, didn't you?" she said quietly.

He licked dry lips. The quietness of her anger was scary. But he was angry too.

"Yes."

"Why?"

He couldn't bring himself to explain about Chloe. So he said, "It isn't right, to take a chain saw to it."

She nodded, controlled, her cold blue eyes surveying the chaos her site had become. "So we leave it, do we? We live in ignorance. We never know how old it is or who built it or why. We let it rot in the wind and the rain."

"It's survived this long. You brought it into the open."

"Do you think I shouldn't have?"

He couldn't say he did. He couldn't say anything.

Suddenly she stabbed a furious finger at the crowd. "Look at them! Living in dreams, in crazy dreams of druids and UFOs and ley lines. Imagining magic in stones, inventing hopeless lunatic theories of star sitings and earth goddesses. These are the people who condemn scientific progress and go home and switch on their computers and e-mail other nutcases just like them. They hate animal experiments, but give them cancer and they'd be screaming for a cure like the rest of us. Hypocrites, all of them! Knowledge is all that keeps us human, and knowledge costs. That's why we walked out of Eden."

"But the Garden of Eden is a myth." Vetch was leaning behind her, one arm on the metal fence. "And we were expelled."

She turned instantly, drawing breath. For a long moment they looked at each other. Then she said, "I *knew* you were behind this."

He smiled sadly. "You've changed, Clare."

"But you're the same." She shook her head. "Still thinking you're immortal."

Vetch looked unhappy. "Don't blame Rob," he said. "There are things at stake here for him you don't know about. And speaking of knowledge, yes, you're right, it costs. It cost us Eden and will cost you the henge, but not the knowledge you mean, of facts and dates. These people you despise want a different knowledge, one that comes from the heart. You remember it. It speaks in myths and stories and dreams. It makes us human."

She snorted. "If the henge isn't removed it will rot here. That's a fact."

"Then it must rot." Vetch looked over at some men in suits climbing the gate. "Death is a part of life. It comes to everything."

"Even you?"

He nodded gravely. "Even me. Fear makes you want to preserve the henge. Fear of losing it. Of seeing it weather down, season by season. Seeing the lichen and the beetles eat it away. But take it out and what have you got? A pile of wood in a tank in some museum. It's unnatural to preserve life at any cost."

"Life!" She laughed. "You talk as if it was alive."

"It is. It's just been sleeping."

They looked at each other. Then she said quietly, "You have changed, Vetch. You look ill."

He laughed, linking his hands so that the three harsh burns were visible. "I'm dying, Goddess," he said simply.

Dark movement slithered around the henge timbers. Rob turned, gasped.

Clare opened her mouth to screech, until Vetch clamped a hand over it.

The snake was long and green. It flowed out from the

timbers of the henge, over the forked entrance, tongue flickering, heading straight for the gap in the metal fence. Rob said, "Is it from—"

"Yes." Vetch glanced behind. "Don't let it get out into the field." Quietly, keeping his voice calm, he said, "Close the gate."

Rob pulled it to. One of the tribe gave a yell, but Rob waved, and when they saw Vetch was there, the men lay down again, snapping open a new beer can.

Against the inside of the fence the snake turned. Its cool scales rippled against the metal; the sound was a fine slithering, a rattle. It moved astonishingly quickly, so that Clare jumped back and Rob felt sweat break out on his spine.

The snake encircled the henge.

Its length amazed them, its thickness.

It took its own tail into its mouth and lay still, one eye unslitted, watching them.

Clare swallowed. She seemed to have no words left, but Vetch murmured, "In Eden too there was a snake—"

"It's not real."

"Touch it. I'm sure you'll find it is."

She bent down, then, hesitant, her fingers went out. Rob stared. She had nerve, he thought. Her fingers reached the snake, and felt its scales. It didn't move. When she drew back, she stood upright and faced Vetch.

He stepped toward her, close, holding her arms. "Goddess—"

"Don't call me that!"

"Clare, then. You know as well as I do where it came from. From the center of the henge, from the tree I have to climb down. From the world you used to believe in, and maybe still do. The world where part of you, the immortal part, is waiting for me."

She shrugged him off angrily, a strand of hair unwinding from her plait. "Leave me alone, Vetch. You've done enough damage." She marched out and closed the gate behind her.

Dan ran up. "Look out."

The police were coming over, and Rosa was with them.

"Police. We're here to arbitrate," the first man said. "All parties need to get together and talk." He glanced at Vetch, but Vetch just smiled calmly back at him.

"There's nothing to talk about," Rosa snapped. "They use a chain saw on this over our dead bodies."

"I'm sure a full and frank discussion will clear the air. Perhaps in the trailer?"

Rosa took a breath to retort and caught Vetch's eye. Slowly, she nodded. "All right. I'll arrange for representatives of all the groups here. But you guard the henge. *Nothing* is done to it until there's an agreement. Right?"

The police officer nodded. Then he looked again at Vetch. "You lead these people, I gather?"

The poet shook his head, amused. He scratched his cheek with frail fingers. "I'm a stranger here. I think you've been misinformed."

"I disagree." Giving Rob a sharp glance, the officer jerked his head at the fence. "Can I see this mysterious henge? It would be helpful to know what all the fuss is about."

Vetch smiled at Clare. She looked horrified, but before she could open her mouth to say no, he had pushed the gate wide.

The policeman stepped in and looked at the timbers. "Fantastic," he muttered.

Rob gazed past him, astonished. There was no snake.

Vetch raised an eyebrow at Clare, then took Rosa's arm and led her away toward the caravan. "We need till moonrise," he said quietly. "Tell everyone to keep it going. Plenty of full and frank discussion, Rosa. Plenty of words. Words are the only weapon we have."

She grinned. "Don't worry, Master. Trust us for that."

Father Mac turned up about seven. Seeing Dan and Rob lounging on the grass, he came over and lowered his heavy body down. "You were all on the evening news. What's the state of play?"

"They're still talking."

"With your druid?"

"Not him. I think he's asleep." Rob nodded toward Vetch's dark shape, curled in a blanket under the trees at the side of the field.

Mac pulled a parcel out of his pocket, waving off mosquitoes. "Brought you some meat pastries."

"I should get back to the pub." Then Dan smelled the pastry and sat back down. "Oh well. Maybe I'll put that out of its misery first."

Across the way, at the trailer, Clare came out. She was red-faced and furious. Flicking one stinging look over at them, she marched around to the lane, flung the gate open, and pushed through the small gathering of journalists.

"Looks like things are not going her way," Mac said drily. He looked at Rob. "You should go home. You weren't there at all yesterday. Your mother will be back."

"Not yet." Rob tied a shoelace that didn't need tying. "Not till ten o'clock."

He knew they exchanged glances over his head. He knew they were worried about him.

"What happens then?"

Dan gulped the last of his pastry. "The moon rises," he said indistinctly.

Father Mac took out a cigarette and a lighter. "God help us," he growled.

By ten to ten the field was dark. Moths crisped and fluttered; beyond the hedge the ripe crop made tiny crackling noises, as if seed was splitting, the whole field releasing the pent-up heat of the afternoon.

Most people had gone. In the trailer the voices argued on. A few die-hard reporters sat in their cars and listened to music.

Dan had rushed off for work. "Don't get arrested," he'd said, joking, and had taken Mac aside and talked to him anxiously. Then, after only a few steps, he'd turned and come back, crouching down, his voice gone serious. "Please go home, Rob."

Rob watched Vetch sit up. "Soon now."

Dan glanced at Mac. The priest shook his head. "I'll stay with him. You get off."

If Vetch had been asleep it hadn't helped him. As he walked over, he looked thinner and paler than ever; he sat very carefully, and Mac said, "You should be in bed."

Vetch shrugged. "I should be home. A matter of minutes, and I will be."

He looked at the tribe around their fires, the dim outlines of hedgerows. Above the trees a faint star glittered. "Everyone's done well," he said. "Very soon now, the moon will come."

Worried, Mac said, "Son, you're sicker than you think. What difference will the moon make?"

"All the difference, Father."

"I'm taking you to a hospital. Right now."

"No."

Mac was on his feet, bulky and ominous. "This has gone on long enough. You need help. You have no home."

Vetch looked down. Then he said, "You've brought something for Rob."

For a moment Mac just stood glaring. Then he took out the diary, looked at it, and sat. He held it out, but when Rob took it, he didn't let it go. "I read a few pages," he said quietly. His expression was grim.

Rob said, "How bad is it?"

The priest pushed it at him. "I should have seen. I should have realized how she felt."

Cold, Rob's fingers closed around the purple book, the silver stars. He wanted to give it back, to push it away. Instead he shoved it into the pocket of his shirt.

A faint rustle and click, from the direction of the henge.

"What was that?" Vetch turned, alert.

They listened. In the stillness distant voices drifted, a radio announcement, flames crackling. Then again, a tiny, rhythmic creak.

Vetch caught his breath. He clutched his side, as if it hurt. "Clare," he whispered.

The night erupted. The creak burst into a shrill whine, high and fierce.

Vetch was up and racing for the henge, Rob behind him; the door of the trailer was flung wide and Rosa came hurtling down the steps, a burly policeman framed in the bright doorway.

The metal gate was locked from the inside. Vetch flung himself against it, hands splayed. "Clare!" He banged it with his fists. "For God's sake! *Clare! Stop!*"

The saw whined, a high electric vibration that went through Rob's teeth and nerves, as if it was Chloe, screaming in terror. He shoved Vetch aside and began kicking at the metal gate. "Get it open!" he yelled. Father Mac was there; his great bulk shuddered and crashed against the fence. It creaked, then all the tribe was on it, howling with rage, pulling and tearing, Rosa kicking furiously at the lock.

In the racket a cell phone shrilled and shrilled.

The gate went down. Vetch jumped over, caught hold of the timbers of the henge and dragged himself in. He turned, white-faced. "Keep them out! All of you. Stay outside!"

Behind him the archaeologists tried to shoulder through; the tribe quickly closed ranks.

Breathless, Rob scrambled after Vetch.

Clare had a small handsaw; it was blade deep in the roots of the central oak. She looked up at them over its whine.

"Turn it off," Vetch begged.

She smiled, cold.

"Is this some sort of revenge? Then take it on me. Please, Clare. Please. On me!" He was devastated, could hardly stand.

Her hair was tied firmly back; her eyes red but dry. "Where are your poems now, then?" she snapped. "All that guff about Gwydion and Merlin you used to spin me? Turn yourself into something, Vetch; enchant me, freeze me with a look. It ought to be easy for you." She glared over his shoulder. "Don't waste your time with him, Rob. He's useless and dangerous. He'll eat up your life with false dreams. He cost me my career once, my life, my inspiration. He ran from me as if he was terrified."

"Clare—"

"Don't move." Her fingers tightened; the blade sliced into the wood with a drone that ached in Rob's bones. "This is *my* discovery, *my* dig. Nobody stops me. If I want a sample I take it, and don't you *dare* tell me I don't care for the henge."

The cell phone. It had been Mac's. Rob knew the call was from the nursing home. He pushed past Vetch and right up to Clare. "You're killing my sister," he breathed.

She stared, amazed, then switched the saw off. In the utter silence she looked at Vetch with hatred. "You've told him that? *I can't believe even you would stoop that low.*"

Vetch moved. Beyond the trees the moon had risen, its full circle lighting his face. Ducking under the tangle of tree roots, he grabbed the saw and pulled it; it switched on and Vetch yelled and leaped back, as if it had cut him.

Tiny flecks of blood spattered the dark wood.

"Rob!" he gasped. Rob jerked Clare's arm. She screamed and the saw fell, whining, churning the mud.

Outside, Mac was thundering, "Rob! We've got to go. We've got to go now! It's Chloe!"

"Hold her," Vetch said, straightening.

"My sister—"

"Hold her." He moved to the tree, put his hands on it, spoke words that were strange and remote.

Clare stopped struggling. "He's mad," she said quietly. "He doesn't care about me or you. He never did."

In the circle of moonlight, the henge was lit. A pool of rain that had gathered in the roots gleamed silver. Tall and black, the timbers enclosed them like a wall of shadow, head high, moths and midges the only movement.

Except that the tree was growing downward.

Rob stared. Out on the field Mac was yelling and shoving everyone aside, but he couldn't move, because the oak was going down and down, its trunk ridged and green with lichen, its boughs and branches sprouting out into darkness, into another place, like a brain stem, like the network of a million cortexes, and a lizard ran up it and slid away, birds squawked in it, disturbed.

Vetch stumbled. He held onto the tree and put his foot on the branches and began to descend, and there was no earth below him, no surface, only darkness that smelled cold and rich, like a forest smells.

After two steps he slipped, weak, leaning his head on the trunk. Rob pushed Clare away and grabbed the poet tight.

"I'm falling," Vetch whispered. He seemed barely able to speak. "Let me fall."

"No. I'm coming with you." Rob began to descend rapidly, pulling the man's feet down, placing his hands.

Vetch's eyes were dark in his pale face. "I can't let you do this—"

"I'm *coming*. I'm coming with you. To find Chloe. Come on! Show me!"

They were climbing down. Branch to branch. Leaves moved against his face, living leaves. Small creatures pattered around him. Vetch's weight slumped against him. Far above, Mac had burst through the crowd, was yelling for him, but there was no sound from up there now but the leaves and the wind. A great wind, roaring and gusting, swaying the branches of the mighty tree, and he clambered and slithered into it, his feet finding holes and forks, slipping on lichen, his toes scraping down and down into greener shadows, the rich decaying stench of a forest.

Into darkness.

Into the Unworld.

The Region
of the
Summer Stars

NG. NGETAL: BROOM

God knows what happened.

There was confusion; the tribe trying to keep us out, and Rob yelling, "Mac!" at me from somewhere, but the cell phone was ringing and of course I had to answer that. It was Sister Mary from the nursing home.

"Father," she said, "it's Chloe—Chloe's arm is bleeding!" Did I know where Katie was?

The woman sounded distracted. I told her we were on our way, rang Katie.

When the police cleared the henge, I barged my way in. Rob had gone. I don't know where he is, but Vetch must be with him.

If they weren't arrested they just seem to have vanished.

The ferocity of the Oak
shook heaven and earth . . .
the Birch, all eager,
comes late in armor.

          ∞ "The Battle of the Trees"

The third castle was revolving.

Gradually, hour by hour, Chloe had come to understand that it was turning, very slowly, like the earth turns. Not that she could feel it underfoot, but if she stood long enough at the window she could see the twilight colors were slowly wheeling over the tops of the trees.

She wrapped the woolen wrap tighter around her shoulders. In this world, the sky didn't change. So it had to be the castle that was revolving.

She turned and paced the long dark room, trying to keep warm.

The army of trees was out there, oak and ash and elm. Tall shadowy shapes. This castle had no shutters, so he'd have to think of something else if they attacked. He was probably off somewhere now, making sure all the doors were locked, the drawbridge up.

Good riddance. The way he fussed over her comfort was infuriating.

But how could a building turn?

Her arm still ached. Somehow in the scramble out from the Glass Castle, she'd cut herself, an agonizing sharp slanting cut that had bled and bled. As they'd run through the deep tunnel she'd wondered if she was leaving a trail of blood drops; the thought had given her an idea.

Now, standing in front of the grimy mirror, she rubbed a hole in the dust and smiled at herself. "Clever girl. Snapped twigs, scuffed trail. Leading straight here."

Behind her the door opened. He came in, carrying a plate of berries and a cup of wine. She groaned and spun around. "I've *told* you. I'm not eating any of that muck."

The mask of ivy leaves looked at her. His eyes darted away quickly. "You must, Chloe. Please."

"No chance. I've read all the stories. One mouthful and I get to stay in your power for all eternity. Well, you can forget it."

He sighed, put the plate on the table and went and sat in the ornate chair by the empty fireplace, crossing his ankles. He wore a clean suit of dark velvet clothes, trimmed with silver. She kicked the stone hearth. "You could light that. It's getting cold."

And that was strange, because ever since she'd been here the forest had been warm, clammy. Before she could think about it he muttered, "How's the cut?"

"Bandaged. With some red silk I found. I think it's stopped bleeding."

The room was silent. She went back to the window, gazing out. Then she turned and faced him. "Something's changed."

"Changed?"

"Someone's trying to find me, aren't they?"

He looked alarmed, glancing out behind her at the darkness of the wood. "Who is?"

"I don't know! I dreamed I saw Rob. I was riding on Callie and I saw him. And then, last time I slept, I woke up because someone was calling me."

He looked back at the fire, his voice brooding. "That was me. There's no one out there."

"There is. I held someone's hand. I felt it, a cold, narrow grip. I shouted and they heard me." He was worried. She knew that. So she made her voice strong and light and carefree. "Maybe they came in through that hole you talked about. I sent messengers, you know."

The mask swiveled. He seemed appalled. "What sort of messengers? That bird?"

"And bats and a snake and moths. Anything."

He stood up, and she knew he was trying to appear calm. "Look, Chloe, you may as well be resigned. There's no way out. I have strong places to hide in. Fortress within fortress. There's no escape from Annwn." At the door he turned. "Stay in this room. I don't want you wandering about."

She smiled spitefully. "Then why not lock me in?"

"You know why!" Exasperated, he looked down at the littered floor. "There aren't any keys. I don't understand where they've all gone."

"So I'll wander where I want and you won't stop me."

He turned, and his eyes were dark and steady through the mask. "You have to make me suffer, don't you, Chloe," he said quietly.

When he had gone, she stood still, a little chastened. For a moment his voice had set off echoes of another place, a time she was beginning to forget. She mustn't let herself forget! Panicky, she fumbled for the chair and let herself down into it, pulling her knees up, hugging them tight. Mum, and Dad, and Mac. Callie, and the girls at school. Even Rob. She mustn't start to forget!

Her hands were shaky, so she pushed them into the pockets of the red dress, and brought out the key.

It was small, and silver.

It was the only key in the castle.

Rob had no idea how long they descended. Leaves smothered him; twigs tugged and snagged, tore at his hair and collar and sleeves. His legs ached; his breath came in gasps, the air thin and tight in his lungs. Small moths and gnats circled; mosquitoes bit; he rubbed sweat from his face with the back of a green-smeared hand.

A little below, climbing unsupported now, Vetch's dark

shape rustled and slipped through foliage. There was no other sound, but Rob knew they were deep in an unimaginably endless forest, that it surrounded them, its rich stink of peaty loam rising up, the mingled unmistakable dampness of fungi and peeling bark and billions of years of leaves.

Then Vetch paused. His voice echoed oddly. "We've reached the bottom branches, Rob. There's quite a jump."

Leaf-rustle.

Then a thud.

Rob let himself down, gripping the trunk with his filthy hands, ducked under the final oak leaves. Vetch was standing knee deep in leaf mold, looking up at him, barely visible in the murk.

"This time I'll catch you, Prince."

"Don't worry. I'm fine." He let go and landed painfully in the soft springy mass, picking himself up.

For a moment they looked at each other. Then Rob stared around.

The trees were dense and silent. A stifling, smothering gloom enclosed him. He had a sense of thousands of square miles of forest, and himself and Vetch tiny things in the heart of it, lost forever. All the green canopy above him was a mesh of branches, of many species of tree, some thick trunked, some spindly, some in bud, some dark with coniferous needles. In the darkness they rustled, as if in a slight breeze, but no draft of wind touched his face. The forest of Annwn was airless and strangely calm. It stank of rot and mildew and lichen and moss.

Vetch sat wearily in the leaves, his back against the trunk. He took out the crane-skin bag, slid a small plastic bottle of mineral water from it and drank. Then he held it up to Rob.

Rob didn't move. "Are we dead?"

"No."

"In a coma? Like Chloe?"

"Not yet. Up there not even a second will have passed." Vetch gestured with the bottle; Rob took it and drank. The water was cold and he was surprisingly thirsty.

The poet smiled, wry. "You shouldn't have come."

"You wouldn't have made it down without me."

"True. I was near death. But that was a second and an eternity ago and far away; we've descended into a world that is mine now, and already it's begun to make me whole again." He stood. In the dimness his hair seemed darker. Rob gave him back the water and Vetch tossed it into the bag. "Besides," he said quietly, "there's no way back. The tree has become one of a million trees, no different. The only way for you now is on, through the caers."

He ducked under a branch and pushed his way through. Rob followed. None of this is real, he thought carefully. None of it exists. It doesn't matter where we go, because in a few hours I'll wake up at home and find none of it ever happened. Maybe not even Chloe's accident.

Vetch was watching. "Stay close to me. The forest holds a million dangers." He turned and struggled on.

Reluctant, the trees let them through. They came down a slope to a stand of birch, then pushed through it to a patch of scrub, where the cover thinned to bushes gleaming with white flowers. Their smell was sickly sweet.

Vetch looked up and smiled. "The summer stars."

Rob recognized them. Very faint, in the purple twilight. Constellations Mac pointed out with the butt of his cigarette on summer nights in the garden with the old telescope. Eridanus, the meandering river. Taurus the Bull, rising late. The Swan. The Girl, Virgo. Brighter than he had ever seen them. Frost-bright, though the wood was warm and mothy.

Vetch turned, listening and breathing. He seemed to be orienting himself; he smelled the air and put a hand on several of the nearest trees. Finally he said, "This way, I think. I don't know how far in we are. Look for signs that people have moved through here. Any traces of a path."

Rob scratched a dried leaf from his hair. "People? Do you mean Chloe?"

"Maybe." Vetch seemed distracted. He was listening; he stopped and looked back, the way they had come. "Did you hear something then?"

Far above, the wind raged. Down here the forest breathed and creaked and rustled around them.

"All sorts of things."

Uneasy, Vetch waited. Then he turned. "Stay close."

They made slow progress. Climbing through the tangled wood was like moving through a world that existed only to hinder them; vines caught at their hands, twigs tripped them. In places the ground sank into vast morasses, the surface virulent with algae, the stumps of drowned trees leaning out like the ruined columns of a palace. Sudden gusts of wind would spring up, plucking at Vetch's coat and Rob's hair; a cascade of golden leaves would spin and spiral and patter, thick as snowfall. Fooled by the dimness, Rob twice put his foot down into bog; the second time he staggered and yelled, almost overbalancing. Only Vetch's grip held him; he dragged himself out and crouched, soaked and scared.

Vetch stood over him. "Some power that's here doesn't want us to get through. I think Chloe is his prisoner."

"His?" Rob looked up, alarmed.

"There have always been kings in the Unworld, Rob. Their names echo in tales. Manawydan, Hades, Arawn, Melwas. The King has many names, but always he cannot live alone. He is darkness and death and winter. He comes up to the world and captures a girl. A girl who is young, alive, beautiful. Like your sister."

"My sister is in a coma in a nursing home," Rob said stubbornly.

Vetch laughed his soft laugh. "This is that coma. This wood." Walking on, his voice came back, echoing from the trees. "When you draw, you copy the world, don't you? You remake it on paper, but it isn't the same. It's yours. No one else could have created it just like that. When I make poems, I use the words we all use, but the order and the sound create a new power. This wood is someone's creation. We stumble through its tendrils, as if we're crawling through the synapses of his mind."

"And you think this King's got Chloe?"

Vetch glanced back. "That's what we have to find out."

They walked for what seemed like an hour, maybe longer. Rob had no way of measuring except by his weariness. Then, on the other side of an alder grove, Vetch walked straight into nothing, and slammed back into the mossy turf in astonishment.

Rob helped him up. "Are you all right?"

The poet rubbed the star mark on his bruised forehead. "I think so." He stepped forward carefully, hands out. Rob saw how his delicate fingers probed the air, found an invisible surface, flattened along it, felt its cracks and blocks.

Stepping back, he looked at an angle. There was a shimmer there, a greenish glint in the gloom. "A wall?" Rob said.

"Caer Wydyr. Glass Castle. The second circle."

"Second? So how many are there?"

"Seven." Vetch looked up. Three shadows hung over him. "She's passed through Royal Caer and this is Glass. The others are Turning Castle, Spiral Castle, Gloomy Castle, the Woven Caer, and the last one, Caer Siddi itself, the Circle of Ice and Fire. Each a fortress, each a level of descent into the mind. At the heart of the seventh is the Chair, the throne of Annwn. Whoever sits in it rules the Unworld." He stepped back. "We need to find the entrance."

They groped around the wall, barely able to see where it was. The trees grew close around and were reflected in it, so the forest seemed unbroken. Rob found he was facing himself, dirty and lichen smeared. His face was small and pale and seemed to have grown younger; it scared him, so he tried to think only about Chloe, about her running to him and hugging him.

Between two ash trees Vetch stopped. "Here. This is it."

They stepped through.

Inside, the castle was cold. The walls were thick and bubbled seams of glass, twisted and fused with palest color, aquamarine and emerald; columns of twisted glass held up shards of the shattered roof.

Vetch scratched the corner of his mouth. "We're too late. They're not here."

The trees had long broken through. They grew in the empty halls, in the vast chambers. Great blocks of glass lay in smashed heaps on the floor; already bramble and bracken were smothering everything. In each room, window shutters had been forced; ragged curtains of foliage hung there now, and a stand of tiny oak saplings had cracked the iridescent paving into tilted slabs and grown a foot high, each with tiny green leaves newly unfurled.

"This damage would have taken years."

"Not necessarily." Vetch scrambled toward a staircase at the back. "Let's go up."

But the staircase was ruined. A vast elm branch had thrust through the wall; its weight had brought the steps down into a confusion of sharp slivers and jagged edges that Vetch kept back from. "Too dangerous. Chloe isn't here."

A breath of warm air.

The faintest chink of sound.

Vetch turned. This time Rob had heard it too. "Someone's there." His heart leaped. "It's Chloe!" He went to run, but the poet's hand grabbed his sleeve and held it tight.

"No. We're being followed. I think we have been since we entered the wood."

"By who?"

Vetch's eyes were dark and troubled; they glanced at him once. Instead of answering he said, "I'm going to make my way back to the great hall. After a few minutes you come too, but loudly, and talking, as if I'm with you. Understand?"

"Yes, but—"

Vetch's fingers loosed from his sleeve. "Just do it. And be ready."

He stepped back. He stepped into the glassy shadows, and at once dissolved into reflections of himself, each shivered and fractured, so that Rob couldn't see for a moment which one he was, and then they were all gone, and something sinuous and lean slipped past him, a dark fox with wet fur that gleamed.

The fox slunk up the corridor.

Rob let out a slow breath. He closed his eyes and saw darkness, licked his lips and tasted the saltiness of sweat and the icy drips from the roof.

He was cold with fear and disbelief.

Far off, something crashed, as if another shutter had fallen. The sound jerked him out of one terror into another; he strode forward quickly, mumbling, saying anything. "Yes, well, all right, we can't go back. Did I ever say I wanted to go back? All I want to do is find her. And you have no right to say I don't!" His voice was rising to anger; he let it. He argued with Vetch, though Vetch wasn't there, because he could never have said these things if he was. "I love Chloe. She's a pain and she always wants attention and she should never have written what she did about me but I still love her. . . . "

He stopped. His hand went to his pocket; felt the small stiff outline of her diary. He hadn't opened it. Was he too afraid to read the rest?

Something crashed ahead.

A gasp, a cry rang out. He turned the corner and raced into the forested hall, tripping over the smashed floor. "Vetch! *Vetch?*"

A figure was inside the door, behind one of the trees. In the glass walls he saw it loom, break, re-form. The figure of a woman, green-stained and worn, her hair coming loose, a stout branch grasped in her hand, and as he watched, she swung it and the fox yelped and gave a great twisting, sideways leap. Wood cracked against glass. The woman screamed in pure fury, whirled to strike again.

"No!" Rob yelled.

She turned, saw him. In seconds, Vetch stood behind

her, breathless. He looked shaken, the whiteness back in his face.

Rob stared in disbelief.

"Clare?" he breathed.

STR. STRAIF: BLACKTHORN

Brain activity has altered. That's what they're saying. Her body temperature has dropped and there's eye movement.

John's on his way and Katie's studio is driving her down the motorway, but it's Rob I'm worried about.

Danny's out looking. He's a good lad.

I should have been around more. I should have been more wary of Vetch. A charmer, full of enticing ideas, and Rob's vulnerable. Always was.

Where in God's name is he?

Chloe's hand is in mine. So small and white.

Into what terrors have I let them fall?

I have been in many shapes
before I reached a handsome form.

∞ "THE BATTLE OF THE TREES"

Vetch had lit a fire, using a tinderbox from the small bag.

The trees seemed to hang over the glow, curious, as if flames and heat had rarely been seen here. Sparks drifted up in the smoke; following them with his eyes, Rob saw the dark interlacings of bole and bough above him, and an owl's white round face peering down. Moths irritated the twilight, landing on his shirt, never still.

The woman who looked like Clare sat with her knees drawn up. She had cleaned her face with her sleeve; now she tied up her hair. But how could it even be her? Because she was wearing a green dress that looked like velvet, and a necklace of berries and seeds.

He said, "How did you get here? Did you follow us down?"

She laughed shortly. "I told you I'd wait at the foot of the tree."

Rob looked at Vetch. The poet was watching the woman warily; his face side-lit with flames and shadows. Now he said, "She is and is not Clare. Here her name is Ceridwen. The vengeful muse, the queen who haunts me. Centuries ago, when I was barely more than a boy, I stole wisdom from her, and inspiration. A crime that made me a poet. A crime all poets commit."

"You stole more than that!" Her voice was fierce. "You stole belief. You stole trust."

He nodded, looking down. "And you won't forgive me. But that's no reason to hurt the boy. The boy is looking for his sister." Sadly, he held a long hand out over the flames. "Can't we forget the past, Goddess? Here, where there is no time? You could help us. With us, you needn't be alone."

She gave him a bold blue glare. "Poets think they know how to persuade. But here, as you say, I have power too. *'I have fled in the shape of a raven,'* you boast in your poems, *'a roebuck, a bristling boar, a grain of wheat. I have been in the dark bag for nine months, rocking on the waters.'* All these abilities you have, Vetch, because you drank them from my Cauldron."

The owl above them flew away, almost silent.

She turned to Rob quickly. "But he's right, none of this is your fault, so I'll tell you what I know. Your sister is in the forest. They passed this way hours ago; by now they will have reached Caer Pedryfan, the Turning Castle."

"They?" he said, his chest tight.

"The King of Annwn has her prisoner. He's always masked; no one sees his face, but he's young and strong."

Rob looked at her through the flames. "Who is he?"

She shrugged. "Only Chloe could tell you."

"Can you take us to this castle?"

"Yes." She spat on her fingers, wiped green lichen from a tree trunk and rubbed it in coils and circles down her face. "I can. I will. But things aren't that simple. You'll need more than me. The trees are involved."

Vetch looked up sharply. "Already?"

"Oak and hazel, birch and thorn. The forest is Annwn, and in it lies death, and hidden meaning. It doesn't stir easily, but it's stirring now, and that must be because of Chloe." She stood lightly. "If you want to find the third caer we should hurry."

Vetch looked at Rob. "Are you tired?"

He shook his head. He felt he should be, because it was twilight, and it felt like years since he had climbed down the endless tree, but though he yawned as he stood, that was just a reaction. He had no feeling of wanting to sleep. Or eat.

Vetch stamped the fire out, scuffing the ashes; the red glow died on the tree trunks around him. Even in the short time of warmth they seemed to have moved closer, Rob thought. "If you don't mind going first," Vetch said mildly. "I'd feel safer."

Clare looked at him with scorn. "We get the boy to the caer," she said. "Then, believe me, Vetch, my time will come. Here I don't need a chain saw to hurt you. Here I am more than Clare, more than a woman you can beguile and desert. Here you fear me. Here I can destroy you, *Poet*."

She turned and strode away.

Rob glanced at Vetch. His face was white.

The room was a small one but it would do. There was nothing to stop him climbing out the window, but it was very high up; propping herself on the sill with her hands, Chloe looked down at the crowding branches outside. He wouldn't risk it out there. The trees terrified him.

Dusting her palms together, she turned back and went into the corridor. She had taken a long time choosing the mirror; there were several in the Turning Castle, but this was full length, and she had prized it out of its ornate frame using a knife he'd left by the fruit.

She picked it up and, struggling with the weight, carried it into the room. Opposite the door was the obvious place, at an angle.

She stood back, looking at her reflection, the doorway, then moved it again, slightly sideways. Perfect.

Now to find out where he was.

She walked silently along the corridor, the long shawl dragging in the dust. There were clothes in all the castles, food, chess games that played themselves, everything she wanted, though it all had a musty, unused feel. Here the dust was thick; she could see his footprints in it, striding toward the stair to the battlements. That's where he would be, up there watching the trees' unstoppable growth. She allowed herself a tight smile.

The plan was a good one and Mac would have liked it. It was always Mac who had read her the stories when he'd come over to babysit. Even now the smell of his cigarettes brought back the picture of the girl lying asleep in the brambled castle. "For God's sake, Mac, you'll suffocate the child," her father used to say, opening the door on the fug.

Of course, Mac was really Rob's godfather, not hers. Hers was her mother's cousin, far off in Ireland, who seemed to have forgotten she even existed. He never sent presents, or rang up to check why she'd missed mass. Mac did. But mostly the presents were for Rob.

She frowned, her hands on the stone wall.

Rob.

She had been trying not to think of him. Now he came surging into her mind, his face, his tallness, the way the girls at school looked at him and giggled if he spoke to them, the way the teachers said *Rob's sister*. Rob's *little* sister.

Rob the golden boy. Rob, who never got the blame for anything, whom they treated like an adult, whose talent always had to come first.

Above all, his wretched paintings.

They were all around the house, seascapes from holidays, the one of Callie looking over the horsebox, one of the stones at Avebury that had won that stupid competition. She hated them all. He'd never done one of her. But then, to be fair, she wouldn't sit still for him.

Resentment made her breathless. No good getting herself worked up.

Get out of here, and then find her way back.

That was the plan.

At the top of the stairs she creaked the small outer door

open and put her eye to the crack. The King had his back to her, standing with his hands spread flat on the battlements, looking out. There was a breeze, very slight. It moved his hair. Above him the stars turned jerkily.

He wore the dark clothes he always wore, a green so dark it was almost black. Rob would know the name for it.

She shivered, almost scared. This had to work. And yet he would be furious. He'd bang and slam against the door, screaming at her, anguished, as he had when she'd pulled the first mask off.

She stepped back, her lips in a tight line. So what? Was she starting to feel sorry for him? That was stupid. Turning, not letting herself think anymore, she ran lightly down to the dark corridor and into the room, lighting the candle she'd left next to the mirror. Leaf shadows moved in dim corners.

She slid the key in the outside of the lock, opening the door wide. Then she squeezed into the dusty niche in the corridor. She took a deep breath. Opened her mouth. And screamed.

Carefully, Clare pushed the branches aside. "There," she breathed.

Rob felt Vetch move up beside him.

The castle was four cornered, built of timber inside two circular ramparts of timber. It was oddly difficult to focus on; it blurred, as if someone had painted it with a wobbly brush full of watercolor, someone not skilled at painting.

"It's moving," he whispered.

Vetch said, "The third caer." He glanced at Clare. "Unbroken."

"You mean the trees haven't broken in?" Rob said quickly. "Chloe's in there?"

"Yes." She nodded, her lips tight. "But look."

Halfway up the palisades, undergrowth was climbing. Ivy and elder, and bushes of gorse and broom. Their spiny yellow branches showed black against the ancient wood; if he watched carefully Rob could almost see them growing.

"Right," Vetch said, "I'll —"

"*No.*" Rob turned. "I'm going in to get her. Not you."

Clare smiled, cool. "That's the way, Rob."

Vetch glared at her. "Rob, this is a dangerous place. You have no idea —"

Before he could finish, a scream rang out from the castle, a high, agonizing scream of terror.

"God!" Rob leaped up. "That's Chloe! What's he doing to her?" Before they could grab him he was running, crashing and ducking through the forest, racing for the gate, slamming up against the roughly shaven palisades, racing around the perimeter furiously. Where was the door? There had to be a door! *There had to be a door.*

The King had his back to her. Breathless, he hurtled into the dim room, stared at her wide-eyed dark reflection. "Chloe! What is it! What —"

Her face moved, vanished. With a gasp he turned, but already she had shoved him back with all her strength, and he stumbled against the mirror and it gave, and as she slammed the door she heard the crash and tumble of furniture.

The little key turned with a snick, just before the whole door shuddered. She leaped back. Her throat felt tight and dry; her heart raced.

"Chloe! Let me out!"

"*No!*" she screamed.

"You can't do this!" He kicked the door, banged at it, threw himself against it. Fascinated, she watched, seeing the ancient wood hold fast, its blackened, warped seams still strong.

Suddenly, he went quiet. His voice, when he spoke again, was tight. "Are you still there?"

To tease him she stayed silent.

"I know you're still there." The whisper was close, as if his lips were against a crack. "Don't go, Chloe. Don't leave the caer. Please. It's not safe out there."

"You would say that."

She almost felt his relief. "I knew you wouldn't leave me."

"I'm going. I'm going right now."

"Wait! They're outside. All around. The trees are dangerous, Chloe. They want to drag me back to their terrible darkness, dissolve me back to the leaves and branches I was made from."

"You, maybe. Not me."

"Are you sure?" His whisper came from the keyhole now. "Why do you think you're here, Chloe? Do you think I abducted you, that I snatched you from the world? They always think that, but you don't know what it's like, to be so alone. I wait and listen, for someone's voice, someone to call me. It was you who did, on that day when you were riding your horse. You wanted me to come and I did, and now I'm protecting you, Chloe. Without me you're alone in the forest, not knowing which way to go, small and frightened. Trust me, Chloe. Please. Open the door."

She was cold. Clutching the shawl tight, she took one step away. His words confused and terrified her. A floorboard creaked; he must have heard it.

"Don't leave me alone again, Chloe!"

She turned her back and ran, racing down the dusty stairs into the hall, grabbing the bag she'd left ready, wrenching the door open to the room where the winch was, to lower the drawbridge. It was huge and ancient, but he'd cleaned it and it worked easily, the chain rattling through by its own weight with a terrible roar that made her jump around in terror. She spun the wooden handle rapidly.

The bridge thudded down. Climbing up into the arrow slit, she looked down.

Then she froze.

Someone was moving out there.

Too vague to see, he flickered out of the wood, a man maybe, in a dark coat.

She leaped back instantly. Were these the enemies he was so terrified of? Was it men he hid from after all, not trees?

She fought for calm. This was the only way out; that was certain, because she'd explored every room of the small caer. The best thing would be to hide. And after they'd searched this room, try to slip out.

The fireplace was immense; they'd certainly look up inside it. There was a brass chest under the window; she ran to it and tugged the lid open and found it was empty.

There was nowhere else. She climbed in, tipped the bag of clothes over her head and lay still, breathless, curled in an agony of fear.

Then she heard footsteps.

Someone was crossing the drawbridge.

R. RUIS: ELDER

They've shunted me out into the corridor while the specialist is with her. "Come on now, Father. Get yourself a cup of coffee."

The sister's a good woman. She keeps looking at the cigarettes, but she says nothing.

I should have been here more often.

That night last month, when I came late and read Chloe one of those old fairy-tale stories. It was so quiet, with just the monitors humming, the words all around her, the branches tapping on the window. An old book I gave her when she was five. She probably hasn't looked at it for years. The briared castle, the sleeping beauty, the beast. Are those stories where she is? Vetch would no doubt say so.

I'm beginning to think our dark druid has gone home.

And taken Rob with him.

Dry your eyes, Prince Elphin.
Too much sorrow will not help you.
∽ THE BOOK OF TALIESIN

When the drawbridge slammed down, Rob had barely leaped out of its way in time; he fell into the overgrown moat in astonishment. Then Clare grabbed his arm and hauled him into the gorse. "Fool! Keep down. Someone might be coming out!"

Cold with sweat, they stared.

The dark gateway remained empty.

Finally, Vetch's whisper came from nearby. "I'm going across."

The poet rustled his way through the undergrowth to the end of the drawbridge and stepped out. In the twilight he was a shadow, tall and dark. He paused, listening, then walked softly across the bridge, his footsteps echoing on the hollow boards.

He ducked under the gateway and vanished.

There was a long silence.

Rob fidgeted. "It may be a trap."

Clare sounded coolly amused. "If it is, it saves me work. But I'm afraid Vetch is only too experienced in surviving."

Rob looked at her sidelong. "You really hate him that much? I think he likes you."

Her blue eyes met his. "Both can happen at once. You love your sister?"

"Of course I do. . . ."

"Just as she loves you."

He was silent. When he answered, his voice was a whisper. "She will when I rescue her. I thought . . ."

Clare smiled sadly. "No, you never thought, Rob. You never noticed. Why should you? She was just little Chloe, doing what she should do. Looking up to you. In awe of you." She moved, rustling the elder flowers. "Until one day something changed."

A whistle.

Vetch had come back out, and was beckoning. Silent, Rob followed Clare across.

"No one in the hall," the poet whispered. "I think they may be up in the west tower. I heard some sort of thud from up there."

Clare nodded. "We need light."

There was a candlestick on the table with seven candles

in it. With Vetch's tinderbox they managed to light it; then he took it in his hand and walked quickly up the stairs, throwing long mingled shadows behind him. Clare followed. Rob came last.

Halfway up he heard a sliver of sound behind him; a draft gusted the flames. He stopped and looked back.

The room beside the gate had its door ajar.

Clare had heard it too. "Go on," she said. "I'll check it."

Vetch's voice was low. "I looked in there. It's empty."

Then Rob heard it, a muffled shout and thump, as if someone was banging on a door above.

"It's her! He's got her locked up."

"Stay here." Vetch turned to Clare. "Go halfway down and watch the stairs. The King may come up behind us."

"And what do you expect me to do if he does?" she said acidly.

"I'm sure you'll deal with him."

"What makes you think I won't join him? Draw him into my revenge?"

Vetch looked at her ruefully. "Goddess, I never know what you might do." He nudged Rob; quietly, they went forward.

The corridor swirled with dust; a dark niche opened opposite a nail-studded door, and a window looked out onto the forest's dark branches, pressed tight against the glass.

Under Rob's feet drips of candle wax had lumped greasily on the floor. "Someone's been standing here." Leaning his head to the wooden planks, he said softly, "Chloe! It's okay. It's me, Rob!"

Silence.

"Can you hear? It's really me."

After a second he looked at Vetch. "She may be gagged," the poet said. Then his face changed, a glimmer of surprise turning into wariness. "Well, well. Look at this."

The key was in the lock, tiny and silver. Vetch glanced back; at the stairs Clare was watching them, her face pale in the candle blaze. He reached out and turned the key.

The lock snicked.

Carefully, holding Rob back, he let the door swing wide.

Chloe raised the lid of the chest an inch and peered through the slit. Whoever had looked into the room had gone; in the hall echoes of voices whispered in the dusty shadows. It sounded as if they were going up the stairs of the west tower. Where *he* was.

She slid out, bundled the clothes back in the bag and slung it over her shoulder. At the door she peered around carefully.

The hall was empty. Quietly, she pattered over the black and white tiles to the shadows of the open gateway.

The drawbridge was smooth and wide; beyond it the forest rustled, the rich smell of its loam and leaves pungent after the mustiness of the empty rooms.

She slid around onto the drawbridge.

It was colder out here. A wind whipped at her long skirt and the shawl, so she tied it tight around her chest and glanced up at the stars. A shiver of sound behind made her turn, alarmed.

The gateway had creaked. Above, blocking the sky, the caer loomed, and she saw it was wooden, a great timber edifice that turned so slowly she could barely see its edge move against the coming night. She turned back to run.

And didn't move.

The trees were nearer.

A living barricade, they had closed off the end of the drawbridge, elder and ash and elm, a vanguard of branches. In their green dimness a flock of birds erupted, scattering in fright. One tendril of ivy encroached stealthily onto the wooden bridge.

She had to go! Right now, at once, or she'd be trapped.

But she couldn't.

Furious, she threw down the bag of clothes and turned to the caer. He was up there, on his own, locked in, unarmed, and she had done that to him. If these enemies of his wanted to kill him he wouldn't stand a chance. She hated him, yes, she despised him, but she didn't want him dead. It was all totally infuriating.

The tendril of ivy wrapped itself around her foot; she stamped on it, and it stayed still. Then she made up her mind.

The only person in the room was a young man.

He was lolling in a chair, one leg over the carved armrest, and he was wearing a mask. Through its slits his eyes watched, challenging and bright. He neither stood nor spoke.

Rob stared in surprise; then stepped in and glanced around the room. A broken mirror, a candle that had rolled out of its holder. Nothing else.

"Where is she?"

He heard Vetch come in behind him; in the dark chamber the candlelight dazzled. Behind the mask the King's eyes narrowed against it. "Who?"

"Chloe! What have you done with her?" Rob grabbed him and hauled him upright. They were the same height.

The King's voice was scornful through the green leaves of the mask. "Maybe I should ask the same of you."

It was a whisper, raw, oddly familiar.

Rob frowned. "Do I know you?"

The King laughed and sat back down. "Chloe knows me."

Angry, Rob said, "Is that why you wear a mask, in case she'll recognize you? If you've hurt her, if you've touched her..."

"What will you do?" the voice asked, amused. "Come riding to her rescue? The knight and the sorcerer. How heroic! But Chloe won't like it. Chloe, I've found, always likes to do things herself. And she won't want you, of all people."

"Why not me?"

The King was grinning. His voice went low, full of mock horror. "Because she despises you, Rob."

Rob went cold. "Liar!"

Vetch's hand gripped his shoulder, hard. "Did she lock you in here?" he said to the masked face.

The King laughed, a mocking sound. "She wouldn't do that, Poet. She and I are friends. I advise you to take her brother back through your Darkhenge and leave us alone, because the truth is Chloe is getting to like the Unworld. Maybe she won't even want to go home."

Chloe was halfway up the stairs when the whisper came from behind her. "I thought it was you who was supposed to be locked up."

She swiveled.

A pretty woman with green swirls on her face stood leaning against the wall. She had blond hair and small pieces of jet and malachite had been threaded through it; they glinted. Chloe liked them. Then she snapped, "Who are you?"

"Now that I admire. Haughty and irritable. You can call me Clare. We're here to rescue you."

Chloe scowled. "I'm perfectly capable of doing things by myself."

"I'm quite sure you are." Clare looked at her thought-fully, then glanced up. Voices murmured in the darkness. "They've opened the door," she said quietly.

"Will they hurt him?"

"I don't think so. Do you want to know who they are?"

"His enemies. He said." Chloe chewed her lip and looked at the woman and said, "I don't suppose . . . we could come to some agreement. Just you and me?"

There was silence. Then, slowly, in the darkness, the woman smiled.

∞

Vetch said, "You know who I am, Winter King?"

"I know. You're Taliesin, the star-browed, the Cauldron-born. Your songs are dangerous to me, but—"

A gasp from the hall below stopped him. Vetch turned. "Goddess?"

There was no answer; he flicked a glance at Rob, thrust the candlestick into his hand. "Stay here."

As soon as he had gone, the King sat up and leaned forward, hands together between his knees. "Did you really think I was keeping her here?" he said earnestly. "You know how headstrong she is."

"You kidnapped her. But she's escaped, hasn't she?"

Behind the mask the King's eyes darkened. Then he reached up and peeled off the mask of green leaves, and Rob's breath choked with fear, until he saw that under the mask was another, of thin birch bark. *How can you escape from yourself?* the dark slit of the mouth whispered.

It blew. The candle flames went out.

Instantly Rob felt a crashing shove in his back. He sprawled forward, saw for a second the flicker of delight in the King's eyes, the candles tumbling and rolling. He tried to gasp, but had no breath; over his head a voice snapped impatiently, "Come on!"

The King gave a great laugh. He leaped past Rob like a dark shadow, grabbed a hand, and was gone.

Rob rolled and staggered up, lurching out into the corridor. "Vetch!" he yelled.

He ran to the stairs, then hurtled down them, tripping headlong at the bottom over a dark heap that lay huddled there.

"Vetch?"

Groping, his fingers found a hand; it was cold. Frantically he searched for a pulse. It was faint and steady, but there was a dark smear too that came off on his fingers. He stared at it, then looked around fearfully.

"Clare?"

No answer. Had she done this? Was this her final revenge, taken at last?

No time to think. He had to get light. Suddenly the darkness of the castle terrified him; he wanted to drag Vetch out into the forest, but would that be right, would that kill him? And how can you die in the Unworld? Does it mean being born somewhere else? Was that why stories never ended? He laughed, a short, hysterical bark, bitten off.

Then he ran upstairs, groped till he had all the candles and thundered back down with them. He felt carefully over the poet's body.

The crane-skin bag was jammed under Vetch's weight. It creaked softly as Rob tugged it out, his fingers sliding inside. He felt something cool, and hard as glass. Something furry, that jerked away. An iciness that couldn't be possible. Tiny cubes that dissolved as he touched them.

Finally, the tinderbox.

He sparked a flame on his third try, and lit the candles.

The flames wavered in the draft from the open gateway; they showed him the empty hall and Vetch. The poet lay awkwardly, one arm flung out, a gash on his head bleeding, but not badly. Now, as if light woke him, his eyelids flickered.

Rob looked around. They needed water.

Reluctantly, he went to the bag again, but hardly had he touched it when Vetch's cool hand grasped his. "No," the poet muttered thickly.

"It"s all right, I don't think you've broken anything but there's a cut on your head—"

"Help me to sit up."

Propped against the bottom stair, Vetch looked haggard. He took a ragged handkerchief from his pocket and the water bottle from the bag, moistened the rag and wiped blood from his temple. He looked at the smear and his face was set.

"Who pushed you?" Rob said.

"I don't know."

"Clare?"

"I don't know! I called her but there was no answer. Then a hand came out and shoved; I went straight down, slammed my head." He turned painfully and looked up into the dark. "Chloe's not here, then?"

Rob rubbed his hands over his face. He sat down and stared into the shadows. "She's gone. So's the King. Someone clouted me from behind too. Maybe Clare. Maybe someone else."

Vetch was watching him intently. "Who was it, Rob?" he said quietly.

Rob shrugged. He wanted to scream, to stand up and switch on a light, to beg for electricity, for the sun to rise. The darkness was beginning to creep inside him, to put out all his old certainties, his beliefs.

"She shouted, 'Come on,' to him. She grabbed his hand."

Vetch didn't have to ask. But Rob said it anyway, just to make himself believe it, to hear the word. "*Chloe*. It was Chloe."

He looked up, his face bleak. "He was telling the truth. He's not keeping her prisoner. She's with him. She doesn't want to be rescued!"

A. ALIM: FIR

"You've got to stop them, Father," she kept saying. "You've got to make sure they don't switch anything off!" She was hysterical almost. And the rest of them, scraggy-looking girls, a few men who hadn't washed for weeks, by the stink.

Vetch's tribe.

"What's it to do with you?" I asked. I was gruff. Katie still hadn't come. Only John, white as a sheet, in there now holding Chloe's hand across the bedding, talking, talking about anything.

The woman said, "He's taken Rob into the Unworld with him. Our people are ringed around the henge. He'll get her out. This is possible. It can be done. You must believe me."

Rosa, her name is. She grabbed my hand.

I let her. I said calmly, "Nothing will be turned off until we know it's too late."

In my pocket, the rosary was twined around my fingers like ivy.

I know why the hill resounds.
∾ THE BOOK OF TALIESIN

The ground was rising, but still marshy. Plumes of gas plopped from it and hung, shimmering with a pale green phosphorescence, stinking of rot. As Rob strode after Vetch, he knew that he was worn with exhaustion and worry, that they had scrambled for hours through stands of oak and rowan, only to reach this place where every growth seemed stunted and dwarfish, twisted in brackish mire.

Since they'd left the caer there had been no sign of Clare. Twice Vetch had turned and called out to her, "Goddess! Please!" But nothing had moved down the long aisles of the wood. Now, deep in mist, Vetch paused for breath. He gasped. "The stars."

The sky seemed closer. The summer constellations hung unmoving, the Milky Way a glimmer. For a moment Rob had no idea what was different; then his heart gave a leap of fear.

Night. From far in the west, darkness was spreading, a real midnight blackness; in his mind, Rob mixed it on the palette. "I thought you said—"

"The Unworld changes. Someone is controlling this." Vetch mused, arms folded. "Rob," he said reluctantly, "why would she want to stay?"

Rob tugged one boot out of the mire. "She's always been a bit . . . stubborn." He thought of her suddenly, of the time they'd been messing around with the radio, each trying to snatch it, and it had got broken. Her blurted, hot rage. *I always get the blame for everything.*

And he had kept quiet, and let it happen.

Vetch was watching. Not wanting to talk, Rob marched on.

Birds were moving. For the first time since entering the Unworld, Rob became aware of its hidden life. A heron flew above the trees, its slow wing flap terrifying. A tiny lizard, black as velvet, streaked across the path.

They walked through a stand of beech, all brown and crisp leaved, into a place where there was grass, soft mossy grass, with tiny closed blue flowers, and bracken.

Trickling through it, shallow and almost silent, clogged with algae and winding water reed, was a small river.

Vetch stopped, waist high in the umbels of cow parsley.

Rob came past him, astonished.

He knew this place.

It was near Silbury Hill, on the banks of the Kennet. When he was small, they'd had picnics here, his mother and him, and Chloe, only a little girl. Jam sandwiches and chips and little cakes from the baker's. Sticky orange juice, striped straws that tangled.

He stood and stared. Three bright yellow plastic plates lay on the grass. On one a silver paper wrapping was crinkled up into a ball. He knelt and picked it up. Next to it a dented Frisbee lay, near the nettle patch Chloe had stung her hand in.

"You recognize this?" Vetch said.

"Of course! It's near Swallowhead Spring." He shook his head. "But there wasn't a forest anywhere near; just a cornfield on the other bank there, and some trees, a hedge —"

"Was Chloe with you?"

"Yes." He was staring at the nettles. They were enormous. Vast spines sprouted from their stems, each with a gleaming pinprick of venom.

Vetch said, "Rob, think. How long ago?"

"About six years. She was . . . six, seven? She stung her hand. . . ."

The poet crossed to the nettles and crouched by them, careful not to touch. "So I see," he said, and at the same time a sound rang out, making them both jerk their heads up. A horn, blowing. Echoing and strange, it boomed over the river.

Vetch turned abruptly. "We're moving through Chloe's mind. Deeper and deeper, as we follow her through the circles of the caers. She remembers this place; that's why it's here. Her clearest memory is of the nettles, which is why they're so enormous. It's a child's terror."

"But it's a real place." Rob nodded toward the willows on the bank. "Just through there, and over the stream, is Silbury."

Without a word, Vetch stood and pushed through the silvery branches.

Rob followed. He almost had to crawl in places, the network of pliant twigs scraping his back. Once, Vetch snagged the crane-skin bag, and tugged it free. Then he wriggled through a screen of leaves.

When Rob emerged after him, the poet was standing a little way ahead.

In front of them, over a lake of crystal clear water, rose a white, gleaming hill, smooth as a seashell. Around its sides crawled a chalk road, rising in terraces.

Vetch nodded, as if he understood. "Spiral Castle," he said.

"You're wrong." Chloe stood up and marched around the crazily tilted room. "I only did it because if they'd hurt you, I would have felt it was my fault. That's all. Blame Mac for lecturing me. He's my godfather. Well, almost my godfather."

In this caer there was no furniture. There were only seashells, vast and in heaps.

The King lay in an enormous oyster, eating cockles with a pin. As always his face was a mystery, but there was no mistaking the satisfaction in his voice.

"The truth is you're beginning to like me. The prisoner always grows to like her captor."

"I'm *not!*" She kicked the shells, wishing there were windows instead of the gleaming mother-of-pearl walls. "I hate you."

"So you'll escape again?"

"I might."

He nodded, then swung his feet down and looked up at her. "If you hadn't come back they would have given me to the forest, Chloe," he said soberly.

"Who were they?" She came and crouched on the floor. "I couldn't see much. The man with the candles had his back to me and the light was dazzling."

"Intruders. They've broken in from above, found a hole that I thought was sealed centuries ago. There are three of them. I call them the Roebuck, the She-hound, and the Plover. Because these are some of the shapes they shift into. In the legends of Annwn they always come when the trees move. They'll try and take you away and lead the trees against me."

She snorted. "The trees seem to be doing a fair job by themselves."

For a moment she sensed his old fear; then he shrugged and settled back into the shiny hollow. "Not here. Here the lake will keep them out."

She stood, one hand on the pearl-smooth wall.

They had crossed the lake in a boat made of what seemed like an enormous yellow plastic cup, with an oar like a bent spoon; there were no bridges, he told her. Then he had drawn the boat up, and before she could stop him, he had taken a stone and smashed a great crack in the bottom, and it had filled with water and sunk with barely a gurgle.

Annoyed, she had stormed in front of him up the chalk path.

It had spiraled around the hill, a white track that soon left her breathless. Wind had gusted against her, stinging her cheeks and bringing tears to her eyes. On each side of the path a border of pearls gleamed, like the double rope Dad had given Mum last Christmas, and between them some small white things that had seemed so puzzlingly familiar she had had to kneel and pick one up. Light, desiccated pieces of crust.

Breadcrumbs?

Coming behind her, he had laughed.

But once at the top, the view had dismayed them both.

As far as she could see in every direction, the forest marched. To the north it rose up to crown a low hill and to the east a ridge, long and narrow. It was as if the Spiral Caer was at the bottom of a shallow bowl of woodland, deep in a cauldron of trees.

Chloe bit her lip. Where was there to escape in all this? But she was determined to keep him unsure of her, so she folded her arms and glared at him. "So where's this castle then?"

Under his mask, he had been smug. "Inside."

The top of the white hill was flat; in its very center a spiral stairway had descended, an exact counterpart to the outside; this also widened as it went down. At first the walls were blocks of smoothed chalk; her fingers had caught their irregularities, the flattened ants and crushed grasses trapped between them. Then the spiraling corridor had begun to gleam; it had been like walking deep inside a vast seashell, like the one on her bedroom window at home, and the whiteness had become iridescent and the steps a long ramp of pearl and creamy shimmer, slippery underfoot.

Finally they had come to this room, seemingly the sole chamber, in the heart of the shell. Circular and windowless, its roof and walls and floor merged into one, vague reflections moving in it. And it wasn't silent either, like the other caers had been; this one hummed, a low, constant hushing, as if around some bend the waves of the sea murmured on a distant beach.

Listening now, she said, "There's no one else in here, is there?"

His head turned sharply. "Of course not. Why?"

"I can hear a voice."

He sat up, both hands on the oyster rim.

She was sure now. Someone was speaking, very far off, very faint. Someone was talking in an endless one-sided conversation, his voice modulating up and down; she could make out questions and intonation, the drone of words, the hiss of esses. Almost she felt that the words were made up of letters that had melted, that were trickling and running down the shimmering chute of the ramp, arriving here hopelessly mixed and heaped, fused into fantastic sounds.

"It's nothing." The King looked around nervously. "Forget it."

Words picked themselves up, put themselves together.

She recognized them: *theater, production ... terrible nuisance really, Chloe ... your mum ...*

Eyes wide, she stared at him. Then she said, "It's my father!"

Vetch crouched at the water's edge and dipped a hand in. Drawing up some of the green weed, he examined it curiously.

"Well?"

"The forest will be able to cross this. Roots will snake out under it, then undergrowth will rise and drown and rise again on the matted remains. But it will take time." He stood, looking at the white spiral ramp of the hill.

"It's Silbury, isn't it?" Rob hugged himself. "This is the downs, lost under all this woodland. These are real places Chloe knows."

"The Unworld is always a real place. And when Darkhenge was made, the downs were forested." Preoccupied, Vetch rummaged through the crane-skin bag; he tipped a pile of rubbish out of it — nuts, berries, a candle, the ogham sticks, the tinderbox, a scatter of ribbons and knotted threads. Quickly he scooped them up and thrust them into his pockets; then, to Rob's surprise, tossed the bag on the water.

"What are you doing?"

The poet folded his arms. "We could swim. *I have been both flesh and fish.*' But why get wet?" He glanced back, into the trees. "Besides, the goddess may be a wolf behind us, or a pike under the surface." He knelt, and put his face close to the rippled water. Softly he said, "I can feel you, Clare. I can hear your heartbeat."

Rob wasn't listening. He was watching the bag as it opened, unfolded, grew to a small skin boat, its thread a trailing rope.

Vetch grabbed it and hauled it in; dragging a straight branch from the woodland, he broke the twigs off to make a pole. Then he climbed in, and held out one hand to Rob.

Rob looked up at the caer, then grasped the poet's cool hand and stepped into the boat. It rocked, and he sat very quickly.

Vetch pushed off. Watching the misty surface warily, he poled them across the crystalline lake.

The King leaped out of the shell. He said nothing. Instead they both listened.

The voice came from unknowable distances. Chloe felt it echoing and whispering through the Spiral Castle as if the whole building was an enormous ear, twisted and fine boned, and she was trapped in a tiny space at its center. Her father's voice was huge. The words seemed too big, as if she had shrunk, or the world she had left was gigantic now, and she could never grow to be a normal size there ever again.

"Make it stop," she muttered.

The King scowled under his mask. "I can't! I told you, the three have opened a hole, a place called Darkhenge."

"What's that got to do with my father?" She turned on him. "He sounds upset. He sounds . . . scared."

He tapped the smooth shell, anxious. "Well, maybe he is. He must miss you."

She stepped forward. "Let me see him."

"I can't."

"You mean you won't!"

"I can't, Chloe! I don't know how."

She put her hands over her ears. "Then make it stop! I don't want to hear him if I can't answer!"

Vetch laughed his soft laugh. Kneeling at the entrance, he upended the crane-skin bag and seeds poured out of it: hazelnuts, acorns, conkers, berries, sloes. They cascaded down as if the bag was still huge; there were far more than it could possibly contain.

Crouched above him, Rob peered down the seashell spiral. "Now what?"

"We go down."

The poet snapped the thread shut, slung the bag over his head and shoulder, and pushed it under his dark coat. He descended three steps, the seeds rolling and crushing under his feet. Looking up, his eyes were dark. "Be ready. They'll be expecting us."

The King said nothing, and when Chloe looked at him he was standing by the tilted lintel of the doorway, and out in the corridor something was rattling. It was slithering and tinkling down the long spiral ramp, and as she took her hands down from her ears and ran over to him it seemed to grow in size, thundering until she felt a vast boulder would roar into the chamber, an avalanche of rock that would bury them both.

"What is it?" she screamed.

He grabbed her arm and pulled her back. "They're still following! They've crossed the water."

With a final mighty rumble the object clattered into the room, rolled across the pearly floor and lay still, inches from Chloe's feet.

She stared down at it. It wasn't huge at all.

It was a tiny black seed.

O. ONN: GORSE

Dan's just rung; he's in his mother's car out on the downs. No sign of Rob. John's hoarse with talking, but now Katie's here. She came running in out of the rain with that blue coat around her; it was just then that the monitors showed the blip.

A small round interruption in the brainwaves.

I went to the window. The trees outside were dripping on the sill, and I leaned my forehead against the cold glass.

Reflected behind me I saw Rosa in the corridor.

I don't know what goes on inside people's minds. I've always tried to know. But there are too many defenses, too many tangles.

Too many masks.

There shall be great darkness.
There shall be a shaking of the mountain.
⁓ "THE BATTLE OF THE TREES"

The King was terrified. He clung to her arm. "Stop them. They'll grow. The forest will grow," he whispered. "Stop them, Chloe!"

How could she stop them?

Every seed was sprouting. And as she watched, an acorn split, sent a pale root splintering into the smooth shell, a shoot unkinking into the air. They grew rapidly, unbelievably. Saplings of every size and species shot up, snapping the chamber floor, cracking it into tilted slabs.

She pulled him back. "Trees can't hurt you!"

"They'll attack now. Our enemies."

"*Your* enemies." She had to shout over the shattering of walls and roof, of leaves unfurling. One of the swiftest trees had reached the roof; with an almighty shudder the smooth mother-of-pearl broke and collapsed. Shards fell, sharp as glass.

"We're finished," he muttered. "There's no way out. You'll have to go with them." He stepped back, away from her, hugging himself. "Go on, Chloe. Leave me here."

She breathed out in frustration, then tucked a stray strand of hair behind her ear. "I'm not leaving you."

His brown eyes stared in astonishment.

"No one," she said firmly, "treats me like a little girl. Not anymore."

"But we're trapped!"

"Rubbish!" She slid back between the thin trunks, twisting under branches. "None of this is real. It's not happening. This is the Unworld. We can change whatever we want to."

He had hold of her arm. "I can't. But maybe you can."

"Me?"

"Quick, Chloe! I can hear them."

So could she. Seeds were splitting and cracking under their feet; the intruders were running down the spiral ramp, two shadows already huge and distorted along the pearly walls.

"Give me your mask," she snapped.

Darkhenge

"What?"

"Give it to me!" She went to snatch it; he stopped her. His hand was cold with damp and sweat. Shaking, he undid the beech mask and held it out; underneath was another, of holly leaves and red berries like one she'd once worn to a Christmas party.

"Right. Now get behind me."

She slipped the mask on. It was warm; the beech bark scratched her cheeks and forehead, its sappy smell rich and cloying, and at once she felt as if she was look-ing out from the heart of one of the trees, as if bark was growing all over and around her, closing her in, a dryad, a creature of twigs and roots. She stepped into shadow, with a sudden conviction that if she kept still no one could find her. And if she didn't speak. Because a tree had no words.

Copying her, the King crouched deep in a holly sapling. She could barely make him out herself.

She took small, tense breaths.

The footsteps raced down the spiral tunnel. Shadows grew, then paused.

A hand came around the corner, a delicate hand, burned three times on the back.

Then she saw the man.

Vetch paused warily at the foot of the curled ramp. In the pearly light his face was paler than ever, the mark on his forehead clear. He reached out and held both arms wide against the walls, blocking Rob's way. "Wait. Something's wrong."

Over his shoulder Rob saw a room of trees. They were so closely meshed they had split the walls and ceiling and were still growing. Branches creaked with tightening pressure; in places shafts of pale moonlight glimmered down from above. Showers of dust fell, light as eggshell, and then fragments of bone white chalk, and soil.

"The roof's going to collapse," he breathed. Then, "Where are they?"

"They're in here," Vetch murmured. "Both of them."

He stepped into the room, circling. Then he reached out and touched the nearest tree with his scarred hand, fingering the bark, the dusty green lichen. He looked up. "Call her, Rob. Call her name."

Inside the mask, Chloe took a sharp breath of astonishment.

Behind the man in the dark coat was a boy. His hair was filthy with mud and his face smeared with lichen. The expensive green top and jeans were snagged and ruined. But she knew who he was.

He turned away from her.

"Chloe! It's Rob! It's all right, we're here. He can't hurt you now, Chloe! We're here to take you back."

She didn't move. She couldn't. She felt as if she had truly rooted, grown into the ground, become a dumb, rigid thing. Her eyes flickered to the King; she could only see the holly mask. Behind its eyeholes was a gleam, barely visible. She knew he was watching her. All she had to do was speak.

All she had to do was say one word.

"They've gone!" Rob's voice was an agony, but Vetch didn't move.

"Not so, Rob." He slid the skin bag from his coat and dipped his hand in, bringing out a thin hazel wand; he began to move into the trees with it, touching each in turn.

"If she was in here she'd answer," Rob snapped. But there was a terrible disbelief in him, because what if it was true, that she hated him, that he was the reason she might not want to go back? For a moment he saw her as she had been for three months, askew in the bed in the nursing home, and then swinging on the swing in the garden when she'd been four or five, small, cute, her hands chubby, her fingers tiny.

He couldn't bear it; he blundered after Vetch.

Into something soft.

As the poet's wand touched the tree, it was not a tree at all, but a girl in a brown dress, a dress that trailed on the floor. Her hair was long and she wore a beechen mask of peeling bark; her fingernails were sharp and painted, her hands hennaed with patterns of leaf and shade. For a moment she was a creature out of some legend; then he knew it was Chloe, and a great sob of relief went through him.

But as he grabbed her, she jerked back.

"Chloe! It's Rob!"

"I know very well who it is." Her voice was flat and scathing.

Shocked, he reached out.

"Don't touch me, Rob," she snapped angrily. "I don't want you here. No one asked you to come." She folded her arms as if barely containing her fury. "You always come and spoil *everything*."

He couldn't believe this. It stunned him. She wasn't relieved, wasn't even pleased to see him. And yet it was just like her. Like Chloe. With a cold shock he realized that something Mac had once warned him of had come true, that over the months of her coma he had made a new Chloe in his mind, a softer, friendlier Chloe, with no tempers or scorn, a Chloe that had never existed, a Chloe that he preferred to the real one.

Confused, he said, "We've come to rescue you."

"I don't want to be rescued."

"Yes you do. You must!"

She glared at him through the mask, an alien creature, her eyes green.

Vetch glanced around; now he reached in and hauled the King out of the holly bush. The King pulled away, then smiled sourly, brushing down his velvet clothes. "Tell them, Chloe," he said. "Tell them you're with me."

"Shut up. All of you!" Then she turned on Vetch. "Am I dead? Is that it?"

The poet's calmness seemed to still her. After a moment he said, "You're not dead." His voice was gentle; he took a step toward her and she didn't back away. "Your body lies in a coma, a long way from here. This is Annwn, where hidden things are clear, where memories surface. Rob has come to take you home."

Impatient, she shrugged. "How long?"

"Three months." Rob's throat was dry; he swallowed. "You were riding Callie. You fell. Near Falkner's Circle. You must remember."

She turned away, arms around herself, so he went on, the words tumbling out now in a breathless rush. "Mum's been frantic, and Dad's turning into a stranger. None of us can face the house, your room, each other. Everything's changed, Chloe. School, church, the whole world. Life's stopped out there, as if nothing grows, as if it's winter in August. We're just marking time till you wake up. We're all waiting for you."

Still she kept her back to him. He glanced at Vetch, who shrugged slightly.

Beside the slowly unfurling holly, the King grinned.

Rob came up behind Chloe. "We thought you were a prisoner."

"I was."

"It doesn't look like that."

She whirled. Through the mask she stared at him, and he was astonished at her anger. "So you want me back, do you? Little Chloe. Girly Chloe. You want me back so your life will be perfect again, and tidy, and just like it was." She smiled, looking at him closely. "I suppose they're all thinking about me all the time now, are they, Rob?

Around my bed, holding my hands, smoothing the hair out of my eyes. That must rankle. That must be annoying you."

He was breathless, silenced with dismay.

Vetch was watching; now the poet said quietly, "You do him a wrong. He loves you."

"Well, I don't love him." Her hands were trembling; she crushed them together. "In this world he can't have whatever he wants. I'll go back if and when I want to."

The King sat down, his back against a trunk, his knees up. He grinned, shaking his head.

She turned on him. "Not because of you, either, so don't think that. But because I'm beginning to see this is my world." She looked back at Vetch, challenging. "It is, isn't it? Mine. This world is me. *I am the forest.*"

He said unhappily, "Chloe—"

"At first I wanted to escape. Sent birds, messages. But I'm growing. I can feel myself . . . my mind . . . spreading out. As if I've escaped from some enclosure, all that bother of growing and hurting and eating and walking and hiding what I feel, even from myself. As if all I used to keep under the surface is bursting up and growing, like the trees." She waved a hennaed hand. "Look at me! I can make anything happen here. I've been a fool not to see that. Watch."

Instantly, all the trees stopped moving. Their constant rustle of growth ended. Rob stared around.

"I did that." Chloe smiled. She spun, arms wide. "Did

you see? I did it. Maybe I can do anything. Why should I go back? I'm sick of being small, and a girl, and the youngest. Here I can do what I want."

"I could force you to," Vetch murmured.

"Yes." The green eyes darted to him through the mask. "You could. You're the dangerous one."

"For God's sake, Chloe, stop this!" Rob couldn't bear it. He pushed past Vetch and grabbed her arm. "We're going. *Now!* And take that stupid mask off!"

He grabbed it; she screamed and shoved him away, but the mask tore and he saw her face, flushed and furious. Crashing into the undergrowth, he fell on his arm and pain shot through him; then he gasped and twisted and kicked. "Vetch!"

The roots were growing around him. Rapidly, swiftly, they snaked under his arms and over his shoulders, forcing him down, whipping around his neck and tightening. He choked, kicked, tried to pull them away, but his hands were full of leaves, tangled bines that wove between his fingers.

"Stop it!" Vetch snapped. He confronted Chloe. "Stop it. Leave him."

She smiled, took a breath. Rob coughed, slumped. He stared at her in amazement, unable to speak, unable to believe.

"We're going." Face to face with Vetch, she smiled coldly. "Get out of my way."

The poet didn't move. His eyes flickered toward the

King, who had closed up behind her like a shadow. The King's fingers came over her shoulder. He held a small berry.

"Take this, Chloe. Eat it. Now, in front of them. Then they'll never be able to take you back, not even the shape-shifter, not even Taliesin himself."

Rob tore the ivy from his throat.

Chloe's hand came up and took the berry. Slowly she held it to her lips, smiling, teasing. "Shall I?" she whispered. "Shall I eat it, Rob?"

He froze. "No. Chloe..."

"I could. That would show them all."

"No. Please. Keep the choice open. Don't close the way back." Vetch's voice was soft, grave. Rob knew he was using it against her, the sounds of the words, the very letters in them. "Please. I know they've hurt you, Chloe. I know it's all inside you, and they've never seen it. I hurt someone like that once, and I think she will never forgive me, never. But imprisoning yourself here isn't the way. Think about it. Take your time."

She looked at him a moment, then slid past him. Vetch backed, making no move to stop her or the King, watching them to the foot of the ramp.

Before she climbed up, Chloe looked back at Rob. She grinned, and waved at him. "See you, Rob. And be careful. I'm only just finding out what I can do."

She put the berry to her lips again, touched it with her tongue, watching him, then the King. Behind the holly mask his eyes were bright.

Chloe giggled. She flung the berry hard at her brother, turned and raced joyfully up the ramp. All the way to the top, they could hear her laughing.

U. UR: HEATHER

"I heard it, Mac." Katie was out of her seat. John turned right around, coming in with coffee.

There was something, but surely not laughter. No one here is likely to be laughing.

Outside, the summer stars hang in the night without moving.

A priest shouldn't be at such a loss. I want Christ to rise into the sky like the sun. I want Chloe to be warmed by him, and sit up and really laugh.

But all I can do is walk over and put my big hands on Katie's shoulders.

Half asleep, she jolts, looks up at me.

"It'll be all right, Mac," she whispers. As if I were the one whose daughter is dying.

Who can measure Annwn?
Or know the extent of its darkness?

~THE BOOK OF TALIESIN

The forest of the Unworld shivered. A ripple and murmur moved through it, disturbing birds. Starlings and thrushes and jackdaws rose, karking and fluttering.

Clare sat at the foot of the poplar, gazing up at them.

Darkness had come. Maybe for the first time in millennia the stars glinted through the dark midnight of the trees, and a breeze gusted, so that loosened leaves fluttered down. Stumps and undergrowth had become shadows, gatherings of mystery. Small rustling movements seemed huge. Moths hatched and danced in the starlight.

She wrapped her arms around her knees, chilled.

Vetch certainly knew she was still hunting him. He always knew. She had spent lifetimes trying to catch up with him, to take back the knowledge he had stolen. As otter and greyhound and hawk and goddess she had pursued him; they had been flames on the marsh, stars that moved silently and infinitely slowly over the skies, grains of corn on a barn floor. In the world above they had played out their fate; she had been a woman called Clare, another echo of herself, another transformation. Remembering, she changed her appearance now, her clothes to faded dungarees, her hair plaited.

In all that time she had never wavered in her fury for revenge.

Until now.

She frowned, rubbing the lichen swirls on her face.

When she had pushed him down the stairs there had been one second of exhilaration, and then terror. As he fell, so violently, gasping and crashing down, utter terror.

For a moment she had been sure she had killed him.

It should have been a triumph. Instead it had been a cold spear in her heart. Her life was a pursuit of him. What would she do if he was gone? As the girl had run up past her she had stood rigid, then raced down and grabbed him, turned him, feeling for his heartbeat, at his chest to hear his breathing.

Relief had swamped her; relief and then fury, because he had made her feel that. Vetch. Gwion. Taliesin. He was her enemy, and she hated him because she could not hate him enough.

It was then she'd had an idea.

The crane-skin bag had lain under him, and she would

have had it then if the boy hadn't come. Now she smiled, and nodded. This time she'd steal it from him. There were other ways of revenge.

Leaves swirled. She looked up, then stood quickly.

Someone was climbing out of the Spiral Castle.

Two dark shapes against the stars, then running down the shell white hill. Clare narrowed her eyes. Chloe and the King. For a moment she wondered how they had escaped, how they would cross the lake; then she saw the smaller one beckon, and with a shiver of tree roots and soil, a causeway squelched up out of the green water, a bridge of dry land. Even from here she could hear how the girl laughed at that, a giggle of delight.

Clare frowned. It seemed the child was beginning to discover how the Unworld worked.

By the time she had walked down to the shore, they were already across, the King like a somber shadow in a new mask of dark holly.

Chloe was grinning; in the gloom she almost walked straight into Clare. "Oh, it's you," she said.

"What have you done?" Clare looked curiously up at the caer; already its whiteness was greening over. Trees were thrusting through its sides. "Where are they?"

"Inside."

"But your brother —"

"Don't talk to me about my brother!" Chloe snapped. "That's my business. He and your druid want me to go back with them but I won't."

"*Won't?*"

"I've told them." She looked flushed, triumphant. Then demanded, "Haven't I?"

The King nodded. He stood under the trees nervously, biting his nails. He glanced at Clare and then down. "It was her own idea," he muttered.

Clare nodded, uneasy. "I see. So you're going farther in?"

The girl shrugged. "Why not?" She jerked her head at the King. "He says there are seven caers, each stronger, and if I can reach the seventh, not even Vetch can force me to go back. No one can."

"That's the heart of the Unworld," the King said earnestly. "The Chair itself."

Clare nodded. "You don't need to tell me. But Vetch will try everything to stop you."

"Not if you deal with him." The girl came up to her eagerly. "I thought that was what you wanted to do."

"I thought so too."

The girl's eyes were bright; starlight glittered in their darkness. "So what went wrong?"

"I don't know."

Chloe looked at her scornfully. "Adults," she said, "are pathetic." She marched away through the marshy hollow of silver birch. The King scrambled behind and Clare followed, noticing how the earth rose up to meet the girl's feet, keeping her dry.

"You say Vetch stole everything from you." Chloe turned abruptly. "Well, that makes him just like Rob. He's stolen from me, though he's too wrapped up in himself even to notice. He stole time, and people's attention from me, and respect, and maybe even love. Just by being bloody Rob. So now I'm stealing all the same things from him. You could do that with Vetch. Couldn't you?"

Clare tucked the ends of hair behind her ears. There was dirt under her nails; the peat of Darkhenge. She cleaned it out thoughtfully.

"I could."

"And that would stop him catching me." Chloe came up to her. Her eyes were bright; leaves drifted into her hair. She smiled a sly smile. "Will you do that, Goddess? That's what he calls you, isn't it? Can I trust you to do better this time?"

Clare didn't answer. Finally she said quietly, "I used to think I was Queen of the Unworld. Now I'm not so sure." She stepped back, chilled at the girl's cool composure.

Chloe narrowed her eyes. Then, deliberately, she touched a twig. A leaf uncurled from it, opened, spread, crinkled, and died, all in seconds. *"Decide,"* she whispered.

Clare stared at the withered fragment. When she spoke again her voice was icy.

"Find the next caer. Leave Vetch to me."

"Oh, that's good." Chloe half turned. "Because if it came to a struggle, I might have to do something bad like that to him. And I wouldn't want to."

She strode away, ducking under branches. The King hurried after her. As he slipped between the trees, he gave one glance back at Clare.

Even with the mask on, the look seemed strangely helpless.

∞

They sat in silence. The shell room was a ruin, the shadows of the trees immense over them.

"I just don't understand it," Rob whispered.

He had said it before. He couldn't stop saying it. His dismay was as difficult to grasp as a slippery snake.

Vetch took a candle stub from the bag and lit it. He dripped wax on a thick root and jammed the candle in. As the yellow light steadied and grew, he said gravely, "You must have known."

"I swear I had no idea!"

"Come on, Rob. Not even from the diary?"

Rob held his breath. Then he put his hand in his pocket and tugged it out. The pages were bent now, the purple felt pen smeared from the forest damp.

He stared at the clotted pages. "I haven't . . . didn't want to read any more."

"Then you should."

He didn't move, so Vetch reached out gently and took the book from him; opening the cover, he separated the damp pages, peeling them apart.

Rob felt he should take it back, that he was betraying Chloe, but then amazement came again in a flood, because who was Chloe? This spiteful creature? The girl in the bed? The toddler on the swing? He was beginning to think he had never known her at all.

Vetch gave him a sideways look. "I think you should hear some of this."

"No," he said, sullen. But Vetch's calm voice was already reading.

"'August thirtieth: Rob's exam results. All As, except Art which was A star. Mum and he are dancing around the kitchen. I want to be SICK—'"

"She's just a jealous kid. . . . Just a kid . . ."

"'April tenth: She's taking him into Swindon tomorrow to buy him a new laptop. They asked me to go but I'm sure they were relieved when I said I was going out on Callie. They didn't really want me around. I had the story all typed up but I didn't want to show it to her while Rob was there. It's worse when he doesn't make fun, when he's earnest and says things like, "Oh that's lovely, Chloe," and then winks at her over my head and when I turn around she's smiling. I hate that. Can't they see? Do they even know I exist?'"

Vetch's dark eyes looked at him over the book.

Rob turned away. His mind was blank; he had no thoughts. There was only a cold dread that had started to creep in, like the tendrils of fog that were rising in the chamber of trees, the damp clouds of his own breath.

Finally he whispered, "What story?"

"It seems she was writing a lot of them." Vetch turned the pages. "Poems too, I'm glad to see, and very good for her age. Imaginative. Spirited. She seems to have been collecting them together." He paused, reluctant. "Then there's this—no date:

I will never, never forgive him.

It was lying on the kitchen table, all ready. Mac had said he wanted to read some—I'd told him part of the plot, and I'd put it there ready. When I heard them all come in I ran down. He'd propped a painting on top of it. They were all standing around admiring it.

I stood at the back and didn't say anything, and then when they'd gone I pulled out my notebook and there was paint on it. Dark green paint. On the cover and soaked into the first three pages, so that you couldn't read them.'"

Helpless, Rob rubbed his hands through his hair.

"'All the words were lost.'" Vetch's voice sounded quietly appalled. Through his misery, Rob shivered. "'All the sounds and meanings, all the words, so carefully chosen. Words that could never fit together again just like that, ever, ever again. And when he came in and saw me crying he said, "Oh, sorry, Chloe. Did your notebook get messed up? I'll get you another one, don't worry." Another notebook. Another girly, pink, fluffy notebook with giggly girly guff inside. That's what he meant. That's what he thought—'"

"All right. All right!—" Rob jumped up and slammed his palm against the bole of an oak. "But I didn't know! How could I know? She never said. She never told me she was writing anything important, anything that meant something!"

Vetch closed the book. "Paintings are easy to see," he said after a moment. "Open, presented flat to the eye. Words are not easy. Words have to be discovered, deep in their pages, deciphered, translated, read. Words are symbols to be encoded, their letters trees in a forest, enmeshed, their tangled meanings never finally picked apart."

In the silence that followed they heard how a soft wind had risen; it gusted and creaked the branches. Rob came and sat down, and put his head in his hands. Vast shadows of himself huddled over the tree trunks.

Finally he said, "You mean this is why she doesn't want to come back."

"Surely."

"All the time. All these years!"

Vetch put the notebook carefully in the crane-skin bag. Then he warmed his hands at the candle. "Listen to me, Rob. You're at fault, yes, for not noticing, but so is she, for not saying. Your gift is the artist's gift, of looking, and it failed you. Hers is in words and she didn't speak them. Your parents may not have wanted to see. But Mac must have known."

Rob tried to think. "Maybe. He always talked a lot to her, asked her about things. School. Friends. Gave her presents. She sort of pretended he was her godfather."

Vetch nodded, his narrow face in shadow. "A wise man, the priest. He would see, but he's no poet."

The room was dark, the candle flame barely glimmering.

"Don't think this is Chloe." The poet looked up at him. "This is her jealousy, her anger. Words refine. Sometimes they simplify. Chloe is asleep in that bed, but here she exists as she might be, without love, without memory. We have to get her back. Even more so now."

Rob wiped his face. "How? She doesn't want to."

"It's worse than that." Vetch looked rueful. "You've seen. She's discovered that the Unworld is hers to control. She'll use it against us. And the King has told her that if she reaches the seventh caer and sits in the Chair at its heart, she will be Queen here. Even I won't be able to take her back."

Rob nodded bleakly. "Then we have to do whatever it takes."

"Good." Vetch stood, and blew the candle out. As soon as he did, they saw night had come. Through the shattered roof of the pearl caer the stars glinted in familiar patterns; the wide constellations of summer, seen through a frost of branches.

Rob shivered. "It's getting colder."

Vetch was listening. "She's brought down a gale."

Outside, the forest threshed. Leaves slapped against Rob's face. "Which way?" he gasped, and then had to shout it again so that Vetch could hear.

The poet pulled him into the shelter of a birch tree. "The fifth caer is a fearsome place. The Black Castle, the Fortress of Gloom. She will have to pass through it, and that won't be easy, even for her. Quickly now."

But the forest had changed; in the darkness it had become an impenetrable confusion of trees and branches. Without Vetch Rob would have been hopelessly lost. But the poet moved purposefully through the tangle of holly and ash and birch, ducking under branches, forcing his way through thickets. In this part of the wildwood the trees crowded densely. Even the rising gale could only roar in the treetops; down below, the air was musty and thick with spores, stinking of rot. Underfoot the leaf drift was so matted Rob sank in ankle deep; fungal growths cracked and splatted under his weight, and when he grasped the trees to steady himself, their bark was so wet it crumbled to sawdust in his fingers. He sneezed, shivered, wiping damp smears of lichen onto his clothes.

Far off, something howled.

Rob stopped. "What was that?"

They listened, breathless in the crackling, roaring wood.

Just as Rob was coming to think he'd imagined it, it rang out again, a high, evil howl, as if a wolf had thrown back its head and was baying to the moon.

Vetch turned and pushed on grimly. "Until now," he muttered, "the forest has been deserted. I fear its inhabitants are beginning to stir."

Down a long hillside they ran, where roots sprawled out of the thin soil in networks of silver, half sliding, half skidding, the soil coming away under their feet and rattling into the darkness below. At the bottom was a small stream; Rob caught the gleam of starlight on its blackness. Cold water splashed as Vetch jumped over, then he soaked his own boot with a shock of iciness. It made him shiver like the shock he carried inside him, that he felt he was running away from, the shock of what Chloe had said, her fury at him. *Well, I don't love him*. Trying to outrun it, he slammed into Vetch, who gasped, "Keep still!"

The poet's thin hand grasped his sleeve and drew him down behind an alder clump. "Listen," he breathed.

Not the howling. But just ahead, through the gusting night, a rhythmic crunch.

Once.

Then again.

Familiar.

Vetch listened to it for a moment. He slid forward. Rob rustled after him.

The night was black. So black and solid it seemed like a wall.

And then he realized it *was* a wall. A wall of inky stones

so smooth the places where they fitted together were impossible to see, and as he lifted his eyes and craned his neck back he realized that it went up so high into the sky that the stars seemed to balance on its top, a vacuum, a wall of nothingness, oily with faint specks of reflected light.

This caer had no door.

And the trees held back from it. Between the edge of the forest and the wall was a rough, splintered stretch of ground, littered with boulders and rubble.

At the foot of the wall, someone was digging.

The chink of the spade was loud; it rang and echoed.

Vetch took a small tense breath, perhaps of relief. Then he stood, and walked out of the trees.

"So here you are," he said.

The digger stopped, and turned. As she lifted her head, she wiped sweat from her smeared face; Rob saw it gleam. Clare leaned on the spade; she looked as worn and hassled as she had at Darkhenge; her plait was undoing and her dungarees were clotted with mud. But she smiled. "Been waiting for you, Vetch."

He stopped.

Mistrust came over him; Rob saw how his eyes moved warily over the rubbled soil. But all he said was, "You pushed me down. In the darkness."

She shrugged. "Do you blame me?"

"You could have killed me."

She turned back to the wall, so they couldn't see her face. "Well, I didn't. There's no way in here. We have to dig under."

Vetch shook his head. "It would take too long." He

looked at her, considering, then up. "Climbing would be better. There will be a door; we can find it."

"No rope."

"I have rope, Goddess." He pulled the strap of the crane-skin bag over his head.

Clare threw down the spade in disgust. "That bag of sorceries gets you through everything. What would you do without it, Vetch?" Her eyes were cold. "I suppose he's told you what it's made of, Rob? The skin of a woman turned into a bird?"

Vetch smiled his sad smile. "Not by me, Goddess." He took one step.

And the trap opened. It opened like a mouth under him, an archaeologist's trench, a goddess's chasm; he gave a great cry and turned, flung himself at the edge, but it was too late; his fingers grasped only leaves, vines, pieces of rock that slithered in and fell under him, crashing to impossible depths.

"Rob!"

Rob was down. Something soft was thrust into his hands, he grabbed again but there was nothing, nothing but the slide and slither of soil, the bounce of rocks, the thud of a body far below.

And the roar of the gale.

On the other side of the wide crack Clare stared at him in fury. "Give that to me."

He leaped up. His heart was thudding in his chest, the bag clutched tight against him. "You finally killed him."

"I very much doubt that. The bag. It's useless to you."

"No." He put his hand inside, found a scatter of small,

soft pieces, whipped them out. In the dark he couldn't see what they were—cloth, or maybe petals, or paper. Light, barely there.

Clare said furiously, "Rob, don't you dare—"

He didn't wait. He opened his hand and the petals streamed out in the gale, a brilliant arc. They wafted up and shimmered and transformed; they became silver coins, and grains of wheat, and feathers and letters and crystals and finally beans, small green beans like the ones in the fairy tale.

Clare screamed in rage.

But the beans hit the ground and grew; they smothered over her in seconds, the stalks streaking up the black wall, and Rob didn't hesitate; he threw himself onto them, grabbing and tugging and finding a foothold, scrambling over her as she ducked, climbing, hauling himself up.

Toward the sky. Toward the stars.

Toward the two tiny faces that stared down at him.

Far up on the summit, high in the cold gale, Chloe turned to the King. "Have you got a weapon?"

He drew the knife reluctantly, the starlight on its blade. Frost crystals formed on it instantly.

She nodded. "Good. I'm going on, and I'm leaving you to stop him. If he manages to get up here, cut the beanstalk."

As she turned, he pleaded, "*Chloe...*" The word made a cloud of icy breath.

It stopped her, but she didn't look back. Only her hair gusted in the gale. Three lanky birds—cranes or herons—

flapped down out of the sky and landed beside her; one squawked through its thin beak. She looked over at it.

"Surely you can do that for me."

The King licked dry lips. "He's your brother. . . ."

She was silent. Then she said coldly, "You heard me. I said, cut him down."

The Battle
of the
Trees

E. EADHA: POPLAR

She came downstairs one day and pushed a notebook into my hand.

"What do you think, Mac?" she said, nervous. It wasn't like Chloe to be nervous.

I don't think any of us had any idea she was writing stories; she kept them secret, up in her room. I lit a cigarette and sat in the armchair and turned the pages—later she complained the paper smelled of smoke.

She has talent. Well, I told her so, but then children's imaginations are vivid. Perhaps her mind is lost in those stories, their transformations and treacheries.

Dan came five minutes ago. A gale's raging on the downs, and there's still no Rob.

As I was talking to him the window slammed so hard we jumped. I went over. The glass had shattered.

It crunched under my feet like diamonds.

Leaves and ivy gusted inside.

*I was with my king
in Heaven's battle,
when Lucifer plunged
to the depths of Hell.*

∾ THE BOOK OF TALIESIN

He climbed grimly, the bag hanging off his shoulder.

The wall was utterly smooth, so there were only the
slithering bines to grip onto, and they were weak, soft,
green growths. But they matted quickly, growing behind
him and twisting in rapid corkscrew movements up his legs,
so that every step was a dragging of his weight out of their
clutches.

He risked a glance down and saw nothing but leaves;
above, stars burned in the sky over the black parapet. He
had to lean his head right back to see it, and that made
him giddy and terrified, so he gripped more tightly and

scrambled faster. Under the frantic sweating of his hands
the new leaves were slippery, icy with frost. They tore,
gave way, came off the black stone in great swathes of
stems.

Gabbling prayers under his breath, his hair in his
eyes, Rob climbed. He knew he was climbing for his life,
that if he stopped, his weight would drag the whole slithering mass away. And the bag was heavy. He hadn't
known that—Vetch carried it so easily—but it hung from
his back as if the forest of the Unworld drew it down,
called it, pulled at it.

He stopped and slung it up, one knee chest high, the
other foot wedged in a clot of branches.

Talons swooped at him.

With a yell he grabbed tight.

A scream rang in his ear.

The bird was huge, an eagle, or some sort of hawk. He
only saw its tail, a flash of one yellow eye, but the gust of it
knocked him against the wall with a bruising smash.

Red bean flowers fell in showers on his face. He
clutched, screamed, "No!"

It had to be Clare. She had transformed herself into it,
a cruel hooked beak that came back again and swooped, so
that he cowered and banged his arm; the bag fell off his
shoulder and slid to his wrist, a bone-breaking weight.
"Vetch!" he screamed. And then, *"Chloe! Help me!"*

Nothing.

From the corner of his eye he saw the bird circle, come
again. He turned his head, flattening his cheek against the

wall, took a breath, let the strap slip, grabbed it, dropped it, grabbed it, and hugged it to his chest, just as the hooked beak dived, the talons flashed.

Pain raked down one wrist in a red slash.

One-handed, he clung to the wall.

If she came again she would knock him off. He would fall. Plummet, far down.

"Rob!"

The voice was just above him. A shape hung out, then an arm, a hand, beckoning and groping. Without hesitation he flung himself up at it, the bines snapping under his weight, hauling himself into the grip that caught his collar, his sleeve, that heaved him head first over the frosted black basalt of the parapet onto a slippery floor of marble.

He rolled, lay gasping.

"Inside!" The King knelt over him, looking anxiously at the sky. "Quickly, before the bird comes back!"

They were on a vast shiny balcony. Behind it a doorway rose, made of three black sarsens, one across the top of the others. They were carved with jagged spirals, and above them the inky wall went on upward, as if it reared through the clouds right into the real world again.

Painfully Rob threw the bag through the dark doorway and scrabbled after it. Like a shadow the King dived after him, rolling inside just before the hawk swooped, screeched, and came to rest on the black stone balustrade.

She sat there.

The raging wind flattened her feathers and lifted them

and flattened them again. Her eyes were remorseless circles of yellow wrath, and she stared unblinking at Rob. He couldn't move.

If it was really Clare she could change again, become some other creature, leap at him.

Why didn't she finish it?

Then, with a suddenness that made him jump, he saw one of the tall shapes on the parapet he had thought were gargoyles move. It turned its head.

One on each side, two cranes stood still, looking at Clare. Their eyes were narrow and slitted, their thin legs scaled. The third alighted with a great flutter, landing on the black marble floor in front of Rob, folding its wide wings. For a moment it looked at him, its graceful neck bending. As tall as he was, it turned to the hawk. It was as if the three cranes were protecting him.

The hawk eyed them coldly. Then it was gone, winging out into the dark, the cranes soaring after it.

Rob breathed out, got up on hands and knees. His wrist throbbed and dripped blood. He felt stretched, all his muscles knots of strain.

Pulling the crane-skin bag toward him, he slid the strap hastily over his head.

The King crouched, watching. In the darkness of the black doorway the wind made an eerie whisper, and it lifted the King's dark hair. He was still wearing the holly mask, but now, as he saw Rob looking, he put his hands up and carefully took it off. Underneath was what Rob had expected, the fifth mask, this time the spiny twigs of blackthorn; the dark eyes looked calmly through the narrow eyeholes.

In his hand, a sharp knife glimmered.

Seeing Rob glance at it, he slid it into his belt. Then he said, "I was going to cut you down."

Rob coughed. Dust clogged his throat. He had to swallow before he could say, "But you didn't."

"I didn't because this is all my fault. You see, I brought her here in the first place. At least, she called me and I came. She was riding the white horse and I drove my carriage right into her world. That's how it should be, how it is in all the tales. Ask Vetch. But she . . . she's taken over. She's so determined, so bitter, that I'm worried now." He shook his head, rueful. "No, not worried. I'm scared. I want you to take her back. I want to help you."

He knelt on one knee under the low passage roof, his velvet clothes stained and worn. "We need to hurry. Where's Vetch?"

Rob bit his lip. "He fell. He may be dead. I don't know."

The King looked dismayed. "We need him! Chloe told Clare to deal with him—probably her plan was to steal the bag that you have. It holds treasures and mysteries; perhaps she believes it holds the lost wisdom he stole from her in the three splashes of the Cauldron. You have it, so she'll pursue you now."

Rob's hand tightened on it. "How do I know I can trust you?"

The King shrugged. "Only you can decide."

That was obvious. But what choice did he have? There was no going back for Vetch. Rob pushed the hair from his eyes. "Take me to Chloe," he whispered.

It was obvious why they called it the Castle of Gloom.

Chloe was on hands and knees now, because the passage—and there was only one—seemed to get narrower and smaller the farther she went. She had the ridiculous feeling that she was getting small along with it, shrinking like something from Alice, crawling along veins and threads of space. And now, when a hole had worn in the red dress and her hands were sore, something was changing. The darkness. She could make out the black stone of the walls, because there was a bend ahead and around the bend came light, a pale glimmer. She hurried, feeling the grit under her palms.

At the bend of the passage she paused, then peered around and stared in astonishment. The tunnel became a corridor, the antiseptic white corridor of some hospital, smelling of disinfectant and floor polish. It was totally real, but still so tiny that the flat fluorescent ceiling lights scraped her back, the second one along sparking and fluttering, as if the strip was going. She didn't feel small now; she felt enormous, as if she had grown to clog the corridor, as if she would be wedged in it, and as she crawled on, she saw tiny doors on each side, and in one of them Mac was speaking, not to her but to some nurse, urgently. Gently, she blew the door shut.

She didn't want him to see her like this.

Just when the corridor seemed to be too small to squeeze through, it turned left, and crawling around she found herself in the hallway of a Victorian house, paneled with oak and hung with portraits, as if she had crawled into an illustration from one of her old books.

Chloe scowled. She was sick of this.

If this was the Unworld, her world, she ought to be able to make it as she wanted. Larger, for instance.

She stopped, closed her eyes. She wished hard, like she wished at Christmastime, or when the exam results were coming out, or when Tom Whelan had talked to her that time in the school cafeteria.

And the hallway moved back.

It swelled up, stood aside. She opened her eyes and found she was sitting on its worn carpet. That her size was normal and she could stand.

There was a table lamp plugged into the wall; she lifted it up and found it was marble and heavy and trembled in her hand, but she could drag it high enough to see the nearest painting. When the light glimmered on the canvas, she laughed sourly at first. And then she stopped laughing.

Clare waited.

It had taken time to escape from the cranes, and she had changed shape more than once. Now, knowing Vetch would survive, would come, she perched high in the branches of the oak. Her eyes were huge, her gaze hungry, her head swiveling in its silent feathers whenever a mouse raced across the forest floor, or a moth gusted in the wind.

When he emerged, her owl sight was ready.

He had chosen well, as he always did. A bat is small and swift, its flight difficult to see, its barely heard echo a squeaky sounding of the forest. She let him fly up, watching him rise from the pit and ascend the black wall, resting sometimes in the withering stalks, then darting out again and circling higher, zigzagging with wild energy across the stars.

When she moved, it was silent. She spread her wings and was gone, and as the bat's weak eyes sensed her, its panic was soundless too, a blundering into the balustrade, a flap between pillars.

She swooped, her vision a wide ring of stark silhouette, her senses full of the stink of the wood, every squirm of her prey, his wriggle and dart, lowering her claws for him, plunging down into the darkness of the castle.

Then suddenly the night rose up and closed around her like an eruption; she gave one squawk of fear, flapped, tore, struggled.

The dark coat was right over her head.

"Goddess, I think we should make a truce," Vetch said quietly.

Rob recognized the corridor. It was the one in the nursing home, the one leading to Chloe's room. He was desperate to know what was happening there, how long in the world's time he had been gone, but though he could hear Mac talking, he couldn't see him, and all the doors had been locked.

Now there was this.

It seemed like the hallway of some Victorian house; he knew it, and it took him a while to remember from where, but then it came, and he said, "Chloe's book!"

"You never read it," the King remarked.

"Not the one she wrote! She has a kid's storybook. Fairy tales. This is from *Beauty and the Beast*. This corridor."

The King nodded. "It would be," he said sadly. He wandered on into the dimness, to the lamp that stood on the table. Looking up, he lifted it. "Rob," he said, "look at this."

Coming up behind, Rob turned cold.

It was one of his paintings. The one of the downs from Windmill Hill, which he had painted in the spring, while Chloe had lain in the grass and sunbathed. Or had she? Hadn't she been writing something . . . hadn't she gone on about it, and he had muttered yes and no and mixed his colors and not listened?

Because now, right across the landscape of sap green and Prussian blue, right down the Chinese white scumbling of the clouds, was a deep gash, a dark, vengeful opening like the one that had swallowed Vetch.

She had slashed the painting into pieces.

With a murmur of pain he ran to the next one, and the next. They were all his work; everything he'd done that was any good, and each had been mutilated, torn, clawed so that the canvas and paper hung down in shreds.

He was so appalled he felt as if it was his own self she had broken open.

The King said, "If we don't get her back, this is how she will be."

Rob turned. His face was white, drained of color. His whole soul was drained of color. He rubbed his dry face, his cracked lips. "What?"

"Trapped here. She'll forget your parents. Her friends. All she will remember is her bitterness...." The King's hands shook as he lowered the lamp. His mask turned, the eyes wet. "I blame myself, Rob. It's my fault."

Rob was silent. He couldn't answer, so he turned and marched on.

The corridor ended abruptly, becoming a place of slabbed stone. The stones were sarsen and they were cold. They made a rough roof, just high enough for him to stand, and led into dimness; on each side, low openings yawned. The ground was uneven with chalk. His breath smoked; the air was chillingly damp, the stones glistening with faint moisture.

As soon as he saw it, he recognized it.

It was the passage of the long barrow at West Kennet, barely a mile from Darkhenge. For a moment he thought with joy he was out, that he was back in the world, but when he turned he saw the King crouched there, and behind him the paneled corridor with its ruined paintings.

Ducking into the first side chamber, Rob saw bones. They lay in a heap, and he knew this must have been how it was before the tomb was excavated, how the remains of its builders had lain here for millennia, sealed in the earth, because he'd read it umpteen times on the notice outside. Skulls and long bones, sorted neatly in piles.

He and Chloe had played in here. Hide and seek. Jumping out and scaring each other.

He drew back, walked on. Two chambers on each side, and then the last, a corbeled roof, the huge slabs of the rounded sides.

He crept into the burial chamber, alert for her yell in his ear, her weight on his back.

It was empty.

And there was no way out.

"Why should I make a truce with you?" Clare stepped back.

Vetch came up to her and held her arms. "Because if we don't, they'll become as we are. Hating, loving, never forgiving. I know how he'll feel, all his life, if she dies. There will be no way he can make it up to her, the neglect, the way he let his art swallow up his life. I know how that feels."

She went to pull back but his grip was firm. "So you should," she whispered.

He smiled. "'*A hen devoured me. I rested nine nights in her womb, a child. I have been dead. I have been alive. I am Taliesin.*'"

Clare looked away. Then, barely heard, she breathed, "For the girl's sake then."

∞

Chloe had dissolved the wall of the burial chamber and made the slabs slide into place behind her. Now she was deep in the forest; it was dark all around her, and she was getting tired of the dark. So she made the moon rise. It came up like a wobbling silver globe behind the trees. That was good.

And she was tired of walking too. The sixth caer might be miles away. So she whistled.

Through the rustling forest a soft clinking answered, and a thud, deep in leaf drift. A white shape detached itself from darkness, vanished, then reappeared between the tree trunks.

Chloe laughed and ducked under the branches, running down a thread of path out into a clearing, where a white horse looked up from grazing, whinnied, and shook its mane.

She gave a great, screeching whoop of joy.

"Callie! Callie, it's you!"

The King said, "We're trapped."

"You're a great help." Rob turned. He looked back up the corridor past the paintings. Then he yelled, "Mac!"

Something rattled and slid.

"MAC! CAN YOU HEAR ME?"

If he could, there was no answer. Only a whine. At first it came from the roof, then it grew louder, emanating from the walls, a deafeningly horrible monotone, a grinding flat line of sound that made Rob clamp his hands over his ears in agony. "What is that? What is that?"

Darkhenge

The King looked around in despair. "A machine. An alarm."

Rob stared at him in disbelief. "Chloe's monitors! Oh my God! *She's making them think she's dying!*"

I. IDHO: YEW

It was Rob. Somewhere close, unmistakable.

"Can you hear me?" he yelled. I was praying, and my eyes jerked wide, but before I could breathe, everything crashed. Breathing, heart rate. We got Katie out, sobbing, screaming. Nurses ran in, carrying pieces of equipment, shoving me back.

I feel heavy and clumsy and useless.

She isn't breathing, she isn't warm. Her face is white and tiny. The line on the monitor is as flat as despair.

They've turned off the alarm, but the silence is worse, and Katie is staring at Rosa, over John's shoulder, knowing their little girl is slipping away.

"Who are all these people, Mac?" she sobs.

There is nothing in which I have not existed.
∞ "THE BATTLE OF THE TREES"

Rob spread his hands against the stones and leaned his forehead on them. "She can't have walked through it."

"Yes she can." The King sat wearily by the puddles on the chalky floor. "To her, this is something to be manipulated. She lives in a world now where everything can be as she wants. Have you any idea how intoxicating that must be?"

Rob didn't want to think. Since the alarm had snapped off, the silence had been too terrifying. "What about us?"

"We're trapped. Unless, of course, there's something in the druid's bag you can use."

Rob hesitated. Then he pulled the bag from around his

neck and opened it, turned it upside down, and shook it.

Nothing.

Baffled, he groped inside. "It's empty! But it was full of stuff. It was heavy!"

The King seemed amused under his mask. "Perhaps the poet keeps his secrets better than we think."

Rob glared. A drip of water fell from the slabbed roof onto his neck, making him jump. Then he said, "What did Clare mean, that it was once a woman's skin?"

The King nodded. "Oh yes, that's true. Her name was Aoife. A sorceress named Iuchra wanted her husband, so she asked Aoife to come swimming with her and then turned her into a crane. The bird flew to the house of the sea lord Manannan, where she lived for two hundred years. And when she died he made a bag from her skin, and in it he placed his treasures. This he gave to the poet."

"Vetch?"

"All poets. Any poet." The King picked it up curiously. "They say that when the tide is full, so is the bag, and when the tide is out the bag is empty."

Rob slammed his hand against the stone. "Great!"

"But in fact it is not quite empty now." The King held it up to him. "Listen."

Taking the soft leather, Rob put his ear to it, half afraid something might come out. At first he heard only the creaking of the leather, and then an undertone of sound, a murmuring. "What is it?"

"Words," the King said. "The bag is full of words."

They were in all languages. Loud, angry arguments and

quiet pleadings, complex explanations and simple prayers. Words that twisted and manipulated and berated and demanded. And through the babble and behind it, there was a music of syllables, as if all the poetry of the world and the Unworld was being recited together, a rosary of crafted sound, each vowel and consonant clear, itself, as individual as the trees in the wood. As if the bag contained a work that never ended, that would go on until something impossible was made, an existence was formed. He found himself thinking of Mac's voice, reading the Christmas gospel among the candles at mass. *In the beginning was the Word.*

He lowered it slowly. "I'm an artist. I don't know about words."

"But the poet isn't here, and we must do what we can." The King stood. "I would suggest you put your hand in, take a handful of sound and meaning, and lift it out."

Feeling lost, Rob put his hand in. There was nothing to lift but he lifted it out, and as it came he felt it slither in his fingers, harden, twist, clatter onto the chalky floor. Briefly the things were ogham sticks, but as they touched the soil they became a cascade of antlers, flint knives, the wide shoulder blades of cattle.

The King groaned and picked one up. "Antler picks. Used to build this tomb, millennia ago."

Rob lifted another and tested it against his palm. The tines were sharp, the grip smooth, as if many hands had honed it. He looked up at the stones of the corbeled roof. "Then we'd better use them too," he said.

∞

It was brilliant to be riding again. She could only gallop if she made the trees stand aside, and that wasn't easy. The trees resisted, they didn't want to do it; they closed up tight again behind her. But for a few moments she let Callie run across the cropped turf of a hill slope, the moon high and full overhead. It was like the downs at night, and there were moths and bats and an owl that flew from tree to tree, and in some places where the ground was low were fireflies, their tiny glimmers lost among bracken and heather.

But keeping the trees away was a strain, and when she forgot, they closed in again, and it was too tiring to stop them. They seemed to be guiding her, forming a long avenue with smooth grass down the center, so that she rode the way they wanted her to ride, always downhill, the wind dying away and a midnight stillness falling on the land.

The sixth caer must lie ahead. She knew that each circle led farther in, and yet each was larger, the forest within it denser. And the wood was not so empty now; creatures were stirring in it. She had heard wolves, and a boar had grunted in a thicket as she passed, its bowed back spined. But that didn't worry her. Why should it? She was Queen of the Unworld.

Rob was far behind. She didn't want to think about him. Clare must have dealt with Vetch. Neither of them would be seriously hurt, surely. And yet she tugged on the reins and drew Callie to a walk, glancing back down the eerie avenue of trees.

Then the enormity of what she had ordered the King to do swept over her like a cold dread. She imagined Rob's terror as the knife slashed the vines, his scream as he fell.

She stopped the horse.

What was happening to her? She put both hands up to her face, felt her cheekbones and eyes, the reins slipping so that Callie cropped the dark grass.

Rob.

She'd always looked up to him. He was older, had always been there, in school, holding her hand on her first day. She remembered how cross she'd been when she realized she'd always be younger, that she'd never catch up with him. How Mum always cut him a bigger slice of cake, because he was a boy.

Stupid things to be jealous of.

But you couldn't kill someone in a world that didn't exist. Could you?

She looked back.

Maybe she should go home. Vetch would know how. And Mac was back there. If she found the Chair in the seventh caer, she would never see Mac again, or Mum or Dad, or the girls at school. Or even Tom Whelan. For a moment anguish filled her up; then the trees rustled in the Unworld breeze, and all their faces faded.

They seemed distant, unreal. Perhaps she had only ever been asleep and dreamed them. Perhaps there was no world out there.

The harness chinked. Callie blew through her nostrils, dipped her head.

Chloe patted her neck and leaned down, rubbing the familiar white coat. "Don't worry. It won't be far now."

If she was Queen, surely she could make the sixth caer come to her.

But when she lifted her head, she saw it at the end of the avenue.

Spun from tree to tree, like a web.

"It's coming! Look out!"

The stone tipped. A shower of soil fell onto Rob's upturned face; he coughed, shook it away, his arms straining up. Heavy on his shoulders, the King's weight made him stagger; the man's fingers dug into the widening crack, forcing the pick in, working it up and down.

Fine gravel crumbled; then with a crack the stone gave. The King hauled it out and tossed it down; he shoved the antler into the gap and pushed, ramming it upward until it went through so suddenly he lurched, and Rob had to stagger sideways to hold him steady.

"We're out!"

Cold wind gusted in.

The hole was tiny; the King's shape filled it. He worked fiercely, tearing down stones and rubble, and Rob gripped his legs and grimaced at the pain in his chest and thought about Clare, how furious she would be at the damage. This was an ancient monument, after all.

But then this was the Unworld, and nothing was the same.

"I can get through now. Push me up."

As the King scrambled and swore and shoved his boots into his face, Rob's worry about Vetch resurfaced. The poet was no longer ill or frail; the Unworld had strengthened him, but it had transformed Clare too, and she was ruthless. What was happening to them?

The King's weight jerked and mercifully lightened; with a sudden slither he was through the hole. After a moment he leaned back through, reaching down. "Right. Pass the bag up first."

"No chance." Rob slipped the strap around his neck. He piled the fallen stones together and climbed, wobbling, onto the heap, squeezing head and shoulders into the gap. The King's voice was rueful. "Suit yourself."

It took an age to get out, being pulled and scrabbling and hauling himself up by his arms, and when he had finally climbed onto the roof of the ruined barrow, he was exhausted, and wanted only to lie on the dark leaf drift and rest.

But the King was urgent. "She's getting away from us. We have to run!"

They ran till they were breathless. The wood had a new, silver glimmer; after a while Rob saw the moon through the dark mesh of treetops. It made things easier, but it had brought out animals, or Chloe had.

The King grew more and more nervous; as they burst through into a place where the trees lined a long track, he drew closer to Rob, grabbed his sleeve, stopped him.

"Be careful. She'll have left traps."

He was right. They found two chasms opening in the ground, as if Chloe had slashed the avenue as she had the paintings, and then a dangerous gushing stream they had to wade across, fast and deep, its bed of chalk and streaming weed.

Once over, they found a strange bogland of tussocks and hollows; it was hard to struggle through, and looking up,

Rob knew that the trees had closed in around it. The King dragged a mired foot from the soft ground and toppled. Rob had to steady him; for a moment they were chest to chest.

"Why don't you take that stupid mask off?" Rob breathed.

He'd thought the King would pull away. Instead his voice came soft and sly. "You do it, Rob. I won't stop you."

Startled, Rob put his hand up to the face of blackthorn. Then he stopped. And drew back.

The King's mouth widened into a smile. "Exactly. *Because you don't want to know who I am.* Who it is that Chloe loves."

"She loves me."

The King shrugged. "Does she?" His face came close to Rob's ear. "She ordered me to cut the beanstalk. With you on it."

"Liar!"

"I'm afraid not. She's not the Chloe you know, Rob, or the one you've invented. This Chloe has never existed before."

A growl, close behind. They both turned.

An animal was squatting under a low bough of oak. Its eyes were small and red, and in the moonlight its muzzle pointed straight at them, intent.

Rob froze. *What is it?* he wanted to whisper, but the King's sudden rigid fear turned him cold; he kept totally still.

The beast yawned.

It stood up and ambled out into the moonlight and became a wolf, huge and silver. The long nose sniffed, the narrow, shrewd eyes moved from Rob to the King, as if it smelled their terror, sensed exactly their inability to run, deliberated between them.

"Listen to me." Rob kept his voice low; even so the

wolf's ears pricked. "Edge closer. We can climb the tree behind me. Move slowly. Don't turn your back on it."

He tugged his foot from the bog. Took one squelchy step. The King was frozen in fear.

"Come on."

"I can't. Not the trees."

"The trees won't —"

"The trees are my enemies. I came from them. They want me back!"

"For God's sake..."

The wolf crouched. Rob didn't wait. He leaped back, felt the tree's hard bark, turned and swung himself up into it, and as soon as his foot thrust into ivy, the night erupted behind him with a great splash. And a terrible scream.

She heard it.

She had dismounted and was leading Callie down the chalk track to the Woven Castle, but the scream made her pause and look back. It was faint and far but she knew who it was. She had got to know his voice, and his fear.

"No," she said petulantly.

A bell rang. It chimed from the structure ahead of her, startling her. Its rich note hung in the frosty stillness, making the cold deeper, freezing her breath, shivering the moonlight into a thing of white beauty.

Was the caer inhabited? None of the others had been. Was it defended?

She looked back up the dark avenue of trees and said, "I

just want them slowed down. I don't want them hurt. Do you understand that?"

The Unworld forest creaked and rustled.

As if it leaned toward her.

As if it listened.

The King's knife slashed wildly; the wolf stood its ground. Its head was low, its snarl ferocious; saliva dripped from its fangs, skin drawn back from the red gums. And in the shadows of the wood Rob was sure there were more, a slinking pack, running in swiftly.

"Come on!" he yelled, cold with fear.

The King turned and ran. He made three steps before the wolf was on him, and another before its weight flattened him on the soft ground. Rolling, he fought it off, but the jaws were snarling, grabbing an arm and shaking, jerking back from the knife.

"Rob!" he screamed. *"Rob!"*

Rob tore the crane-skin bag off and hurled it down, then threw himself after it. He landed hard, falling forward on his hands, pain in his side.

Kicking out, he screamed and yelled at the beast; it leaped back, growling, and he grabbed the King, straddling him, heaving him up. "Move!"

Dragging the torn arm over his shoulder, he ran with the stumbling man, but there was no way, he knew, of getting him into the tree.

Gray bark reared; he turned, his back slammed against it.

Together, they faced the wolf.

Well, it wasn't like the other caers.

There were no walls, or at least not solid ones. It was a castle made of rope, or what seemed like rope; vast thick skeins of looped stuff, twisted and slightly fuzzy to touch, hanging from trees and posts and timber pillars, making a honeycomb of openings and tunnels.

The colors too were varied. In most places it seemed red but there were flecks of blue and yellow and green. It was like wool magnified a hundred times, a knitted castle, matted fibers under a microscope.

There were so many openings she had no idea which to choose; this caer was a labyrinth. As she hesitated, the bell chimed again, deep inside, this time more urgent.

Chloe bit her lip. This wasn't right. Whichever way she chose would be the right way, because this was her world. She was the writer of the story. Choosing an entrance, she led Callie into it, but after only a few steps four or five dark red openings led off in different directions, and she could see through the openwork walls. It was utterly confusing.

"Now what!" she snapped.

The answer came from behind her, though there had been no one there.

"This is how it is for poets. Always choosing and selecting."

She turned, icy with fury.

He was leaning in a loop of the stuff, as if it was a swing, like the one in her garden at home.... His face was dark but she recognized the star mark on his forehead.

The three scars on his hands.

OI. OINDLE: SPINDLE

It's as if she's fighting us.

They've got the heart going again, and there's still brain activity, but this shouldn't be happening. Even looking at her face, I can see a change.

"Chloe," Katie says. "Chloe?" She bends down and kisses her on the forehead.

Are there places too far away even for love to reach?

Behind spines and thorns and briars?

I won't believe that.

I will never believe that.

*Though I am small, I have fought
in the ranks of the forest.*

∽ "THE BATTLE OF THE TREES"

R ob had never had to fight.

In school he had always been popular, not one of those who got picked on. He was tall and had always been absorbed in his art, and though he'd once done a term of martial arts classes, the real thing had never happened.

Besides, this was an animal. It had no mercy, no fear.

It wouldn't hesitate.

Rob felt the weight on his arm ease; the King pulled himself straighter.

The wolf paced toward them, head low. Its ears were flat,

its teeth yellow. When it leaped, the impact would be staggering, its bite would rip through muscle and bone.

He searched under his coat. Then flicked one despairing
glance sideways.

The crane-skin bag lay under the trees, where he had
tossed it.

He inched a foot toward it. The wolf's hackles rose, the
growl deepening in its throat.

And to his astonishment the tree bent down between
them. At least that was what he thought was happening; then
with a flash of understanding he saw one dark bird had
landed on the branches above, its weight bending them. Then
another, and a third.

Long-legged, thin-billed, the three silent cranes perched
in the branches. In the dimness they gleamed pale. The King
whispered, "The *guardians*," his voice a cracked breath of
hope.

The cranes looked at the wolf.

Doubtfully, its amber eyes moved from Rob, surveyed
the birds.

Nothing moved.

And then with a crashing of branches they could hear
something approaching through the icy forest, its weight
vibrating the ground. Something vast, something enormous, something that cracked and splintered its way
through the undergrowth, so that Rob flattened his back
even harder against the tree, wishing it would open, wishing there was a doorway inside it that would open and swallow him.

The wolf slunk back. Its teeth were still bared but its eyes darted in fear.

To the left, a thicket of blackthorn trembled. A shadow shouldered through, leaves and berries dropping from it, soil sliding from it, as if it had reared itself up from some mud hollow.

A great horned head, a dark pelt, rain-soaked, two tiny red baleful eyes.

A bull.

"Quietly." It was Clare's whisper. Rob felt a hand grab his, pull him gently behind the tree. The King seemed transfixed; Rob had to tug at him urgently before he stumbled, and at the movement the three cranes all swiveled their beaks and looked down, fixing him with their gaze.

Clare drew him around the bole of the gnarled oak into the dimness behind, but even as they moved the bull lumbered forward, dropping its head. Its mouth opened like a pit of darkness; it bellowed, a terrifying roar of defiance, advancing on the wolf.

The wolf snarled, but it was slinking, its belly low, its ears flat.

Then it turned, and ran.

"She's totally useless." Chloe folded her arms in fury. "Twice now she's supposed to have stopped you, and yet here you are."

Vetch nodded mildly. "It's gone on longer than you think."

"And you brought Rob here. Of all people!" Without waiting for him she turned and marched into one of the looped openings, holding Callie's harness tight. The horse's bulk was warm and comforting, her flank steaming slightly after the swift ride, but even behind the thud of hooves Chloe felt Vetch's presence stride after her like a shadow.

"You won't slow me down," she said angrily. "I'm going to the Chair. I'm going as far in as I can get." She glanced back and saw how his dark eyes watched her, irritatingly calm. "I could kill you," she said. "I could make you die, just by wanting it."

"Perhaps you could," he said. "But you won't."

She walked faster, but he was tall, and kept up easily. Ducking under skeins of the flecked ceiling, she said, "Out there I was small and weak. Have you any idea what it's like to be a little girl? I didn't have any power, but that's different here. The King told me about the Chair. Whoever sits on it holds all the power of the Unworld. Was he lying to me?"

"If this world is yours," Vetch remarked, "you could make such a chair, couldn't you? *If* it is. But have you thought, Chloe, that in fact it may not be?"

She stopped, dragging Callie around. Vetch was a little breathless, but then so was she. "No I haven't! I don't believe that. You're full of tricks and lies and stories. You never tell the straight truth."

He smiled ruefully. "Now that's unkind, coming from

you." Taking a step forward, he put his hand on Callie's slender neck and smoothed her mane. The horse whickered, nestling up to him. "Because you never do either, do you? You pretended, but you were bitter in secret. Rob, your parents—you never really told them how you felt."

He was looking down at her; she felt humiliated. "What was the point? I couldn't explain."

"Then how can you blame them for not knowing?"

"I do! I blame Rob." She wished she was older, taller. She wished she knew how to argue, how to be logical, how to use words back at him. Tears choked her; she swallowed them, turned, marched on.

The thick wool grew tangled. She had to step over it, duck under it, draw Callie around vast impenetrable knots that blocked the way; she strode fiercely through openings and gaps, taking any way that seemed open, and all the time Vetch came behind, silent, as if he was biding his time.

She wanted to race away from him, but the castle tripped her and snagged her; it looped around wrist and ankle. Denser now, it closed in, growing colder, as if she was forcing her way to the heart of the mesh. Small things began to scuttle past, always running outward; they looked like mice and spiders and beetles, and once a snake, wriggling in panic. And the tunnels weren't still either. Sometimes they rose under her feet, or twisted, or even rippled, so that she and Vetch and the horse all lost their footing and staggered against the stretchy, yielding threads.

And then Vetch began to talk.

His words were quiet, and though she wanted to block them out, she couldn't.

"It's not easy, is it, to find your way through? Yet it should be, if this Unworld is yours. But have you thought, Chloe, that it's you that's hindering yourself?"

"Shut up," she snapped.

"Tripping yourself up, tangling yourself? That we're struggling deeper into your own doubt? That secretly, far down somewhere inside, you don't want to get to the Chair at all. You want to be stopped. You want to be made to go back, to wake up safe in your bed and see Mac leaning over you, and your mum and dad crying with joy. You want to make it up with Rob. You want it to be all right."

"I said, *shut up!* You don't know anything! Rob's dead. *I've killed him.*" She turned, hot and hurt and desperate not to hear him, flung out a fist at him. He grabbed it, and his hand was cool, the marks of his theft three red coils on his pale skin.

"No you haven't."

"What do you know?"

"I know about the struggle with words. *About 'The Battle of the Trees.'*"

For a moment she just stared at him. Through him. Saw a white room full of nurses, Mac in the background looking sick and old, a broken window where the ivy was creeping in. Felt a small cool kiss on her forehead.

For a moment she was there and wanted to be there.

And then she saw the painting. It was on the wall, behind Mac. It was brilliant, it was beautiful, it was hateful. It was her own face, the portrait she'd always wanted Rob to paint, which he must have done since she'd left; it looked down at her with that light, mischievous grin she fell into sometimes, when things were good, when she could forget about being their Chloe, and be her own.

It hurt her. It stung tears into her eyes.

Vetch recognized the change. He looked dismayed.

She shook his hand off and stabbed a finger at him. "That's enough! No more words!"

Red rope dropped around him; he dragged it from his lips. "Don't! Chloe, wait..."

Around his neck, another loop. It tightened; he choked, tore at it, but his arms were held, his wrists dragged back.

She stepped up close to him. "No more words, Vetch. Now you're the one who's tangled. See how you like being speechless. I'm going on."

She turned Callie and strode away.

Vetch fought. He struggled and pulled at the red-flecked ropes, but they held him and slithered around him and crushed his chest. He was suffocating in them; as she climbed up on Callie's back, Chloe said without turning her head, "That's enough."

The threads were still.

Vetch tried to loosen them. He said, "You know I'm right. My words will go with you."

She smiled at him kindly. "It'll take you long enough to

get out of there. Good-bye, Vetch. I'm sorry you won't see me reach the Chair. Any of you."

"We made a truce," Clare said sourly. She held a whippy branch aside for Rob; before them the hillside ran down, the grass smooth. "He's gone on to find her; I came for you. She's on horseback, so we've got no time to talk."

Rob looked back. "But . . . the bull. Those birds."

"Guardians of the crane-skin bag. There are many such magical beasts in the wood. I brought the bull because I couldn't deal with the wolf myself." She smiled a tight smile. "Chloe may think the Unworld is hers, but it isn't yet. There are powers here stronger than she is, until she reaches the Chair." She turned then, and he saw with dismay that she had the crane-skin bag.

It hung on its string around her neck. Now she took out a single ogham stick and held it up like a wand.

"I'm afraid I have to change you."

Rob said, "That's Vetch's. What do you mean, *change*?" Alarm flooded him; he said, "I don't want —"

"I'm sorry, Rob. It will hurt a little, but it's necessary." She tapped his face, then the King's, quickly, and as he looked he saw the King's mask alter. The blackthorn leaves shriveled, the eyes widened, became round; tufts of feathers sprouted.

And then he felt it himself, the contraction within him, the sudden gasping agony that made his eyes water. He knew that his body was twisting, that his mind was collapsing, all its thoughts and reason folding away, leaving only light and pain and hunger and fear.

His bones hollowed, his skull attenuated, his hands clawed.

And then he lifted himself up from the ground.

And flew away.

This caer. She had no idea what it was called. She galloped away from Vetch's imprisoned shape quickly, ignored his hoarse plea. "What good is a queen without subjects, Chloe?" he yelled.

The tunnels narrowed. Red and warm. She rode faster into veins and blood vessels. Flocks of birds flew against her, a scatter of scarlet moths, a swarm of bees.

Far ahead, the bell chimed, and then a clattering grew clearer. It sounded like the clack of great needles, as if someone was knitting the castle, as if stitches were being formed and slipped and counted in some enormous chamber ahead.

But all she found when she finally burst through the last knot was a room she knew very well indeed.

Her bedroom at home.

It was exactly the same, except that the bed here was all made of antler, and bones, and rough branches tied together, with four posts of dark wood inside a ring of high, unshaven timbers.

She slithered down from Callie's hot back, and looked around.

Her wardrobe. She could change, and wash.

Her clock. The small hands said 4:50 AM.

Her photograph of Mum and Dad and Rob on holiday.

Her notebook.

Suddenly, she was so tired. She sat on the bed and it was soft and full of feathers. The duvet was white, embroidered all over with snowflakes; it wasn't hers, but she liked it.

She drew it around herself, and it was warm, and smelled sweet, so she curled up, kicked her boots off and yawned.

A small sleep wouldn't matter.

And Rob was alive.

Smiling, she touched one of the embroidered flakes with her fingers, watching it detach and float up, letting sleep open under her.

Vetch gasped a ragged breath, then another. He had managed to wriggle his long fingers up to his throat; now he rubbed it and swallowed, feeling the red soreness of the tight threads.

He was shaking.

To discover the uselessness of words was too terrible a fate for a poet.

A small wetness stung his hand. Then another. He looked up quickly, his breath smoking, and despair chilled him to the bone.

He had failed to persuade Chloe. And now she was making sure they never caught up with her.

For through all the interstices and webs of the Woven Castle, through all the hollows and loops and tunnels, small white flakes were falling.

Snow.

UI. UILLEAND: HONEYSUCKLE

In the corridor, Dan's sitting with Rosa. I wonder how she's explaining her idea of where Rob is. And Vetch.

It's 4:50 AM.

Her eyes are slits. Outside it's raining. John is standing at the window, shredding ivy. On the floor are petals of honeysuckle, sweet and wet. "Look at this, Mac," he says dully.

Three great birds, like herons, have perched up on the next-door roof. Their narrow eyes look down at me, and somehow, they're a comfort.

Beyond, like a dark ridge, the downs rise over the town.

And I can sense Vetch, his irritating calm....

Vetch is close.

But he may be finally lost for words.

I was at the fortress
when the trees and shrubs marched . . .
∽ "The Battle of the Trees"

Someone was flying. Rob realized it was him.

His body was a creaking, lightweight framework, jointed in impossible places. He was streamlined, and currents of cold air moved above and below him, and he banked and tilted on them, as if they were solid.

Far down, lost deep inside a tiny skull, his mind looked out through wide-angled eyes, saw a concave hemisphere, its colors muted and new and unnamed. Were there words for the colors only birds could see, or the instinctive lift and balance of feathers on the wind?

In Vetch's druid bag, maybe. Nowhere else.

Ahead flew a hawk and a white owl, who had once had names. He had no name either, but was a floppy-winged creature, green-sheened, with a quill of feathers. He searched for words and they came, but from another life far away, lying in the grass, birdwatching on the downs with Mac. Plover. He was a plover.

Snow stung him. He realized it had been snowing for a long time, a swirling whiteness that was frosting the air and almost obliterating the forest below. But through gaps, between gusts, he could see enough.

He could see that the forest was on the move.

Did it walk? Or did it just grow? He sensed its progress, the swift, purposeful surge toward the east, a million slithers and rustles and strides. There were beasts down there, migrating or fleeing; glimpses of strange-skinned creatures among the massed trees, birds that swooped and circled in flocks above the impenetrable canopy.

But it was the trees that were terrifying. Ancient oak and flimsy hawthorn, coppery stands of beech, stocky elms, streaming in movement. All the hedgerow growth, elder and blackthorn and ivy and gnarled apple. Willows along the banks of invisible streams. Rank on rank of conifer, dark armies of fir and pine and spruce.

From this height he saw that the landscape they invaded was his own landscape, the Wiltshire hills that he knew as green and sheep shorn, smothered now under the primeval forest, as it must have been centuries ago, before Darkhenge was made; that secret wildwood of shadows and magic animals, of outlawed men who lived like beasts. The forest that was mankind's enemy and the place where his imagination was born, that he destroyed and dreamed of, burned and built in, cut down and made of its timbers entrances back into himself.

A draft from the hawk's swoop tipped him.

Below, he saw a structure in the wood, a tormented red castle, its shape mystifying. The hawk began to drop toward it, circling deftly down eddies of snow. Carefully, the owl and the plover followed, descending through sleeting showers.

Nearer, the caer gleamed. Frozen in loops and hollows, its red wool hung with icicles. Snow swirled through its openwork tunnels. It seemed deserted.

When Chloe woke, the duvet was far too heavy and yet the room was as cold as ice. Sitting up, she felt a weight of snow slide off her and slump wetly to the floor. Shivering, she stared around.

A blizzard was howling outside. Here the dark-timbered bed had filled up with snow; it crusted the wardrobe and her dressing table, dusted the picture frame, filled the slippers that poked out from under the stool. She breathed out a cloud of dismay.

How long had she been asleep?

She had to hurry! Leaping out, she heaved the warped

door of the wardrobe open and tugged out clothes. They weren't hers. A white dress trimmed with fur, a great coat of ermine, boots. There was a muff too, and a fur hat; giggling, she pulled them on, feeling like some Cossack or the Snow Queen.

Then she hurried Callie back out into the latticework of tunnels.

They were clogged with snow. Furious, she stamped her foot and soft powder dusted her new clothes. Vetch was wrong! She wasn't doing this. She *wanted* to get on, to the last caer, but it was as if something else was always holding her back. She'd ride hard now, and not stop till she reached it. She'd sort out this mess.

"No more snow!"

She said it firmly, commanding. Still flakes fell, tiny and deadly.

"I said, no more. That's it. STOP."

But it didn't stop. It fell with a gentle insolence, and the realization turned her cold. The weather was not obeying her. *She was losing control.*

She wanted to scream into a tantrum but couldn't; she felt chilled, and subdued, as if while she had slept another part of her had been forgotten. Instead she climbed onto Callie and paced through the frozen mesh. Once she looked back, hearing something shiver, and tinkle, thinking Vetch had come after her. She almost wanted him to be there. But only the red tunnel twisted into dimness, snow falling through it.

She was alone. And though she told herself not to be stupid, she knew she was scared. She wished the King would catch up with her. He was her only friend now. Had he left her because of what she'd asked him to do? Had she pushed him too far?

It took a while to find a passage that was clear, and when she did, it led into a place where the red threads had been wound around a network of dark timbers, weaving in and out of them to form a high wattled fence, higher than she could see over. She walked the horse around it, curious. The entrance was on the far side, a thin gap, that you'd have to turn sideways to squeeze through.

An eye slit. Would she?

She drew Callie to a halt, and had almost decided to dismount and take a look when, from inside the structure, the bell rang.

It was so loud!

She put her hands to her ears; with a shudder, Callie reared up, and Chloe had to grab at the reins in panic. All through the Woven Caer the echoes of the great chime vibrated; icicles fell like daggers, birds fluttered, the whole frail structure trembled, slid, began to collapse.

Instantly Chloe kicked her heels in and urged the horse into speed. Ears flat, Callie galloped, leaping snowdrifts and tangles of wool, her rider hanging on low under the drooping roof, not knowing where they were going, until with a sudden emergence into moonlight they were out,

The Battle of the Trees

racing over a broad white downland under the perfect circle of the moon.

Hauling the snorting horse around, Chloe stared back.

Silently, without speed, the Woven Caer was crumpling. It fell inward softly, imploding and springing back like a great pile of fibers.

Snow settled on it and guilt shot through her like the stab of a knife. Had she left Vetch to smother in there?

Before she could think of it a hawk swooped out of the snow, straight into her face.

Chloe screamed and ducked.

The bird was fast; it dived and veered off, but it was the second attack that caught her, a green plover that came straight at her head so that she lost balance, and with a scream of terror fell off into the drift, hands out.

She fell into snow and yet into some past where the snow was chalk and hard and there was a black car skewed across the lane, and people running and running toward her. A car horn blared. Her fingers bled onto chalk and flint.

"NO!" she screamed. "I won't remember! I won't!"

Shaken, she scrambled up. Callie was shivering, blowing smoky breaths of fear, her eyes white. The birds rose, swooped, screeched down.

Chloe ran.

Vetch had got his hands and half his body free when the bell rang. As soon as he heard it he knew what it was, so when the owl flew down and turned into the King, staggering dizzily against him, he shoved the masked figure off impatiently. "The bag. Do you have it?"

"Clare does."

Vetch said, *"What?"*

"Too hard to explain." The King's fingers worked at the knots and tangles hopelessly. "I'll never get all this undone! The castle is collapsing!"

Vetch looked grim. "I know that. Keep still."

"But—"

"Keep still!" It was hard like this. From so far away. He gripped the frozen red strands hard with his left hand, put the thumb of the right to his mouth and bit. A tiny fleck of blood welled up through his skin; he tasted its salt, quickly closed his eyes.

Far away, in other worlds, through dreams and nightmares, heroes walked.

One of them was powerful, a giant. In the darkness of his mind Vetch made the words come, made them strong. Strong enough to cross distances of silence and mistrust.

"Mac. Mac, listen to me. I need you. I need your help."

Chloe struggled. She forced her way, waist deep, up the smooth snow slope, tearing a ragged gash in its beauty. Ahead of her the banks rose, immense and shining, a rampart of snow and chalk, the Ice Caer, the seventh fortress, Caer Siddi itself. Behind, like an inexorable shadow, the forest pursued her, sending out roots and tendrils to trip her, and tug at her, and she screamed and fought with fury against the clogging drifts.

The snow was another betrayal. It seemed hard and then crumpled, its surface crunching.

However she struggled, the forest was faster. It loomed behind her, over her. Its shadow darkened her. And as she scrambled and tugged her boots out and hauled herself up to the caer, the hawk and the plover came down right in front of her; she dodged around them, plunging for the dark, narrow gap of sky that was the entrance ahead.

"Chloe! Chloe! It's me. It's Rob."

She stopped.

He was standing right behind her, but she didn't turn. She didn't move at all.

"I'm sorry." The snow creaked. "About all of it. I didn't know how you felt. Maybe, back there, you didn't know either."

"And that makes it all right?" Now she turned.

The trees were lined up behind him. Clare was there too, looking tired and bedraggled. Chloe smiled at her sourly. "You've gone over to them, I see. All of you are against me now."

She folded her arms inside the muff, pleased at how Rob shivered in his ridiculous summer clothes. "Well, you listen to this. I've come this far. I'm going inside the caer. For once I'm going to do something that I want to do, decide something all for myself, with no one else telling me. Can you understand that, Rob?"

He looked at her. She was so assured, so strange across the snow.

"I can understand that, Chloe," he whispered.

I. IPHIN: PINE

I turned and grabbed it all. The knitting, the cell phone, Rob's painting off the wall.

Katie jumped up; John stared. "Mac, for God's sake..."

I flung the door open, dumping all the stuff into the corridor. "Dan! Rosa! Get in here."

The music went off, the cuddly toys went out. We cleared the place. A white, gleaming emptiness. Then I slammed the door and wedged a chair against it.

Bells exploded into panic. A nurse thumped outside. I folded my arms and looked at Rosa.

"This is it. Now we pray. Your druid needs our help."

We formed a ring around Chloe, holding one another.

A dark circle.

As I struggled for breath inspiration saved me.
Heaven's lord would set me free.

∞ THE BOOK OF TALIESIN

Chloe ran into the entrance, Rob and Clare behind her like shadows.

Before them, the vast interior gusted with snow. This caer had no roof but the sky, and that was lost in the blinding drifts. Its ditch was water-filled and frozen. On each side, huge as petrified giants, great stones rose, a stark, blunt ring of them, snow settling in their holes and crevices.

They all knew this place. This was Avebury henge, the great circle as it must once have been before its village cluttered it, and roads divided it.

Between the enormous entrance stones Chloe trudged

purposefully, sinking knee deep into the snow, and as Rob followed her in, he saw that a ring of fire had been lit, great balefires crackling between the stones. Outside, the trees gathered. All around the great bank they closed in, a besieging force hundreds of miles deep, a black rustling army pressed tight, and out of them creatures slunk, fox and otter and hare and bear, climbing the bank, outlined against the moon. He thought he saw people come out and stand there too, ancient hunters with spears, as well as Marcus and Jimmy, all the tribe with their fluttering colored banners planted in the chalk, as on the day he had hauled Vetch into the circle.

Dan climbed up, and Chloe's friends from school, and his mum and dad, and Mac, his arms folded, looking disapproving, and yet in the blizzard they blurred and thinned, as if whoever's mind it was that had brought them here was barely strong enough to hold them to this place.

Chloe said nothing. Her face was set in a cold white control that scared him, and she struggled forward without looking around.

Clare muttered, "Vetch isn't here."

"He'll come."

She glanced at Rob sideways, sour. "You trust him too much."

"I like him. Mac liked him." That surprised him. He hadn't even known he knew.

Chloe crossed a second ring of fires and reached the central circle; the southern one, with its odd row of smaller stones, and in the center a mighty obelisk.

Rob stared up at it in awe. Thin and leaning, its blue shadow stretched over the snow. A third flame ring surrounded it, the flames lapping the stones, so that there was only one entrance, a narrow gap. Chloe stopped. Her shadows, hundreds of them, flickered and leaped.

She turned. "This is it, Rob."

His heart jumped. "Chloe, I can't go back without you. I won't."

She smiled ruefully. "Yes you can. Because you got used to it, didn't you? Me lying there. Me being so still. You got so used to it you were starting to think I wouldn't wake. Even that it would be better that way."

"Yes!" Furious, hot tears in his eyes, he marched up and yelled in her face. "Yes I did! All right! I did! I didn't know that's what I was thinking, but I was, and who can blame me! I had to protect myself, Chloe, had to build a fortress around me. Day by day a few more stones. Because it would have been unbearable otherwise."

Shocked, she stared at him.

"And Mum was doing it, and Dad and Mac, we were all hardening at the edges and that's okay! That's normal! It didn't mean we'd given up! It didn't mean we didn't love you."

A movement to his left. He saw Clare glance over quickly.

The blizzard stopped.

It stopped so abruptly they were all surprised; their breath clouded the clear air. Above them cloud streamed away; the stars were suddenly burning, the strange constellations of the Unworld, fiercest blues and reds.

And within the circle, they saw that the tall stone was the immense backrest of a chair. The seat itself was a horizontal slab, and over it lay a length of red cloth, each corner weighted with a small hanging golden apple. On each side a single twisted hazel tree grew, heavy with nuts, and before the throne a well opened in the ground, a small round circle of water, reflecting the stars.

Chloe took a step toward it.

"Chloe!"

To everyone's astonishment the voice was Mac's. He was climbing awkwardly down from the bank and was walking forward between the stones, his bulk more solid with each step. Rob felt overwhelming relief, joy like a sudden weakness behind his knees.

Chloe stared in dismay. "How did you get here?"

Mac shrugged. "Vetch is a little . . . tied up. He asked me to have a word." Reaching into his pocket, he drew out the cigarettes and familiar lighter. Striking the flame, he bent his head to it. "Well, not just me," he said indistinctly.

Chloe looked around.

They were coming down from the bank, a tribe of men and women in crazy-colored clothes, and Dan trailing behind them, giving her a weak grin. "Hi, Chloe," he said nervously.

"This is mad. I didn't bring you!" She felt panic rise; fought it down. "Don't come any closer, any of you. You're not really here. You're back there."

"And so are you." Mac blew the cigarette smoke out gratefully. "Lying still and crooked with your mum and dad beside you going through agonies. I never thought, girl, that you'd do that to them. I never thought you could treat us all with such contempt."

Tears sparked in her eyes. His rebukes had always hurt her; when she spoke she knew her voice was small. "I'm not. It's just—"

"Pure self-indulgence." Mac looked around at the vast stones. "Seems to me I know this place. You could have used the church, Chloe, for your inmost caer." He looked behind her at the Chair. "Though that looks vaguely familiar."

She couldn't bear this scorn. "I only ever wanted you to think as much of me as you do of Rob!"

Mac pointed a stubby finger at her. "Not true. Jealousy, Chloe, that's what this is. A deadly sin. Don't fool yourself." His voice softened. "And I do love you, you silly girl, as much as Rob. We all do."

"There you are. *Silly girl.* That's how you think of me, Mac, and even you can't see it."

That silenced him. She saw him grimace.

After a moment he said, "I'm sorry, Chloe. What you say may be true. And it's true I feel I have a responsibility to Rob—I am his godfather and that's important. Maybe it means you've lost out. But if you want me, I'll be yours too from now on. If any of us remember any of this." He hesitated, throwing the cigarette down and grinding it under his heel. Then he looked up. "There's a forest like an army out there. But I think we could bring your mum and dad through it, if you—"

"No." She shook her head firmly, taking off the white muff and crumpling it in her hands. "No thanks, Mac." She was suddenly sure she would cry. It was rising up inside her; what a fool she'd look, before all these people, and up there on the bank, all the kids from school.

She glanced at the Chair. "If I sat there I could send all of you away."

Clare said, "Could you?" Tucking her muddy hair back, she came and caught Chloe's arm.

Chloe pulled away, irritated. "Get off me."

"I know what you're thinking. You think if you sit there you'll rule the Unworld. I thought that too. But people can still hurt you, Chloe, they still will. There is nowhere in this world or any other where you can hide from them."

"I'm not hiding—"

"That's exactly what you're doing. I know what it is to take refuge in revenge. Spending eternities damaging yourself, just for the sake of seeing him hurt." She stepped back, watching the girl carefully. "But if you go back and face things, you can change them."

Stubborn, Chloe snapped, "Everyone always thinks they know best—"

"We do," Mac growled.

Rob edged a step closer. There was one way he could stop her. If he could get past her, he could sit in the Chair himself. But a flicker of doubt came and went, the thought of Chloe and his parents without him, and it must have shown on his face, because with a gasp of anger she turned from him and ran, dodging Mac, sliding between the fires.

"*No!*" Rob yelled.

Something shoved past him, a musky-smelling roebuck, its flank iced with sweat. Between Chloe and the Chair it ran, and shivered into a man in a dark coat, breathless and weary. Before she could stop herself Chloe ran right into his arms. She screamed and kicked in fury; Vetch held her tight.

"You won't stop me!"

"I know I won't." Vetch sounded worn; he forced her to turn her head. "He will."

Rob spun in surprise.

The King of the Unworld stood behind them in the circle. He wore his final mask, of ice and silver birch, and in the red light it was a shimmer, and his face and hands and clothes were garish in the heat and scorch. Sparks rose from the flames behind him.

"It's me, Chloe," he said sadly.

"You!" She stepped toward him; Vetch kept hold of one wrist. "You were the one who brought me here in the first place!" She tipped her head, trying to see him clearly through the smolder. "Why did you do that? Who are you?"

He came forward. And as he reached out and took her fingers they saw that his hands were crusted with bark, his nails gnarled and lichened. Small threads of root clung to his clothes.

"I didn't bring you. You called me and I came for you, and I wanted you to stay. You know who I am, Chloe, because you dreamed of me, put me together from all the words and syllables you know. That's what poets do. They make people out of sound and images. Out of leaves and seeds."

The Battle of the Trees

She stepped back, eyes wide.

He smiled. *"You made me from the forest, Chloe.* I'm anything your imagination wants me to be."

Vetch let her go. Carefully, and very slowly, she reached out to lift off the King's last mask. He stood still, letting her, his eyes dark behind the silver. Her fingers touched the icy bark. Then, as if she feared what she might find beneath, she pulled her hands back.

He smiled at her.

"Do you still want me to stay?" Chloe whispered, "Won't you be all alone without me?"

The King said, "I want you to make your own choice."

She looked at him, then turned to Rob, and Mac. "What about you?"

"He's right," Mac said unexpectedly. His voice was a rasp of pain. "Decide, girl."

Rob couldn't look at her. His face was hot; when he raised his eyes he could only see how much she had grown, how much she looked like him.

"Rob?"

He nodded, silent.

Chloe turned to Vetch. The poet said gently, "You see, you do have power. Words give you power, to create or destroy." His eyes flickered to Clare. "Even to forgive. Be generous to yourself, Chloe. Go home."

She sighed, then walked around him to the Chair.

None of them moved. She gazed down at the velvet seat and Rob knew that she could sit there now if she wanted to, that none of them could stop her; that she could settle herself back against the cold stone, and raise her hands and command the weather and the words and the Unworld.

They had come to the seventh caer, and the decision was hers.

AE. PHAGOS: BEECH

The machines are silent.
We are a dark ring around the bed,
a forest of trees.
Neither of mother or father
were we made,
not our body or our blood.
But of nine kinds of elements,
of God's fruits of Paradise,
of the flowers of the primrose,
the blossom of trees and bushes.
From the earth's roots we rose,
from the broom and the nettle,
from the water of the ninth wave.
The Wisest One made us in
the earth's dawn,
knowing what the stars know
before Time, before the World.

Under the root of the tongue
is where the battle is fought.
The war is won
In the mind's mazes.

        ∞ "THE BATTLE OF THE TREES"

There was something strange about the Chair. For a start the snow didn't settle on it. And from the tree on the left as she watched, a hazelnut slipped and fell, plopping into the darkness of the pool. In the water a fish moved, a flicker under the surface.

Behind her Vetch said, "The waters of Wisdom."

"I could drink some of that?"

"If it helps."

She knelt and scooped up a handful; it was brackish, peaty water, dark with fibers. As she sipped it, it drained from her palm. It tasted cold, and of nothing.

Then she straightened, walked to the Chair, and touched the red velvet seat. When she turned, it was to face the ring of silent faces.

This wasn't right, she thought. There should be something now, some panic, some adventure that would startle her, that would make her see her life with new eyes. An attack from the outside that would save her from having to decide.

They were all here. The trees, the people.

She could make it happen.

Almost as she thought it, Rob gasped. Over her shoulder he glimpsed movement; he yelled, "Vetch!"

Vetch raised his head.

Beyond the stones, over the high banks, the forest had invaded.

Trees shot up, cast a cannonade of acorns and chestnuts, hazelnuts, berries. As soon as they touched the soil they split, sprouted, grew. Roots unsprawled, branches rustled out, uncoiling twigs and leaves. With rustling, horribly accelerated slithers and groans, the wildwood crawled over the henge, gathered, darkened the stars, closed overhead. As it thickened, the moon dimmed; the watchers on the bank were swallowed by it.

Mac swore. "Stop this, girl!"

"It's not me, Mac, I swear!"

The henge had a green roof. Acorns and conkers and sloes dropped from it. Squirrels ran rustling from stone to tree.

"It's not me!" This was the panic she had asked for, but she couldn't control it, the wild fear of the wood, what it contained. She turned to Vetch and he caught her hands as they reached out for him. "I wanted power, I always wanted it, but it's stronger than I am! I can't control the Unworld, Vetch, or the real world either. I can't make it do what I want! The forest is too strong."

Vetch crouched, his narrow face close to hers. "You will, Chloe. I promise you." He glanced at Mac. "Ask him. God gives no one a gift he cannot master. Right, Priest?"

Mac growled. But he said, "Right."

Then, turning swiftly, Vetch held out his hand to Clare. "Give me back the bag, Goddess."

She looked at him, unsmiling. "Why should I?"

"Because they mustn't end up as we did, tormenting each other down the years."

Clare looked at him, her eyes blue and clear. For a moment Rob thought she would turn and go, into the dark entanglement of the wood. Instead, she did something that astonished him.

She stepped past Vetch, and past Chloe, and walked around the pool.

As oak leaves wreathed above her, she sat on the red velvet of the Chair.

Instantly the forest halted.

Clare looked up. Three lanky cranes fluttered down and alighted, one on the chair back, two on the narrow strip of grass. Their long beaks snapped and clattered.

Clare said, "I'm sorry, Chloe. But this is my place and I resume it. I am Ceridwen here, Queen of the Seven Caers, always and forever the muse of all poets." Her hand reached out, and from her forefinger hung the small crane-skin bag.

Vetch took it. His eyes met hers, and though he said nothing, Rob knew something had passed between them, something had changed, had dissolved. Then the poet turned and held the bag out to Chloe.

She seemed confused. "What's that?"

"It contains everything you need, Chloe." Vetch came close. *"Words."*

"I've got plenty of words."

"Not like these. These are the ogham letters of the druids, the secret runes of the trees. The roots of language, Chloe, the seeds of story. Everything grows from them, all the worlds you want to make. They make peace and start wars, they burn cities, they wound and stab, they heal. They're the only way we have of making others understand our lives, how it feels to be a man, a woman, a boy, a little girl. While we have them we can shape-shift, we are never trapped in our own souls, our own skin." He smiled, reached out, and opened her small hand, crumpling the bag into it. "There are a million Unworlds here in this bag, universes uncreated, races unborn. Take it, Chloe. Hang it around your neck. No one will see it, no one will be able to take it from you in all the years you live, not Rob, or Mac, your parents, any husband you may have, any children. Only you'll know. All your life, the secret gift the trees have given you will be there."

For a moment she didn't move. She seemed small beside him, suddenly bedraggled and tired. When her hand closed around the soft leather it seemed heavy for a moment; her arm dipped as if there was a weight there that was too much for her.

"What about you?" she breathed. "What will you do?"

His eyes were dark. He said, "I've found my muse. She will have to do."

Chloe looked at Clare, who nodded.

Then Chloe slipped the cord around her neck.

Vetch smiled. Under his dark hair the star mark on his forehead shone. He took her hand and led her to Mac.

Mac touched her hair gently. "Time to go, Chloe."

She was biting her thumbnail, something small girls did, something Rob had not seen her do for so many months it brought him a stab of joy and terror; then she turned to him, her voice weary.

"I'm really sorry, Rob."

Shaken, he said, "There's nothing—"

"Yes there is. Not saying. Being jealous."

He shook his head, any answer choked up. "You look tired."

"I am." She laughed a little laugh. "As if I'd stayed up long past my bedtime." Looking up at him, she fingered the cord around her neck, and he was suddenly reminded of Christmases when she was small, the early morning frantic opening of presents, the satisfaction, the sleepiness that came after.

He put his arms around her, and she didn't flinch.

"Let's go home, Rob," she said quietly.

Over her head he looked at Vetch. The poet was leaning on the back of the Chair, his hand on Clare's shoulder, and to

Rob's amazement the blond woman reached up and touched his scarred skin, even though they watched Chloe, both of them, absorbed.

Rob said, "I don't know how."

"I do." It was the King who spoke. "You must climb, of course." Pushing Rob gently aside, he put his hands around Chloe's waist. "Are you ready, my lady?"

She looked at him closely, then gave him a shy kiss on the brittle mask. "I won't forget you," she whispered.

The King laughed sadly. "Ah, but you will. Though you'll search all through the poet's bag to find me again. And one day, perhaps, among the echoes and images, among the tales, something will seem familiar." Easily, he lifted her, her white dress drifting against him, hoisting her up into the green canopy of acorns and hawthorn. Chloe grabbed a branch, and stepped up onto another.

She climbed, quick and agile.

She didn't look back.

"Wait for me!" Rob scrambled after her into the foliage, looking down to see Ceridwen's upturned face, and Vetch's calm smile.

"Will you be . . . Will I see you again?"

Ceridwen shrugged. "The Cauldron-born cross many worlds. We live in yours, just as we live here. Part of me will be in Clare still. But hurry, Rob. The sun's rising."

He nodded, glanced once at Vetch and looked for Mac, but the priest was no longer there. Instead, streaming from the east, light was breaking into the Unworld. Brilliant, horizontal, the lazy red fire of the dawn shot through the trees. As

Rob climbed quickly, he felt it warm him, knew a slit had widened, as if somewhere an eye was opening, and the slushy drifts of snow slithered and melted and fell wetly on his face.

Leaves surrounded him. There was no sound from above but a rustle that might be Chloe or might be birds; he called again, "Wait for me!" but there was no answer, and the tree trunks rose around him like dark timbers, an enclosing circle that he was climbing up through the center of, and the boughs of the tree were black, fossilized with age, pitted and cracked with time.

He was climbing the highest tree in the forest, and he came out above the canopy, and swung there, and saw all the Unworld below, in its sunrise.

Then he reached up, and touched the sky.

The sky was warm. It was soft as cloud. It licked his face and nudged itself against him, and then it snuffled and scratched ferociously at its fleas.

It also stank.

Rob lay quite still. When he opened his eyes he saw, inches in front of them, the gnarled smooth wood of Darkhenge. A spider was making its careful way over a dewdrop, tickling his cheek. As he breathed out, the web spun from his face to the timber quivered.

Tearing it, he sat up quickly, grabbing the upturned tree.

He was soaked, and shivering. The dog gave a short bark of displeasure, then shook itself, sending drips flying.

He was lying inside Darkhenge. Chips of wood scattered the enclosure, and the chainsaw notch in the central trunk looked raw. Rob caught hold of it and pulled himself up, staggering slightly. He was winded, as if he'd run a long way. Putting his feet down carefully, he pulled himself along to the entrance and stared out.

The field was empty, except for litter.

It looked like the aftermath of a rock festival. Bottles and cans glinted in the grass. Abandoned banners were soaked with dew; the rising sun lit the letters of SAVE DARKHENGE with a golden glow.

"Hey!"

A policeman was crossing toward him. "Where the hell did you come from? I thought we cleared everyone out."

Rob rubbed his face. He was desperate with thirst. "I fell asleep. Look, I need a phone. It's an emergency."

"There's one in that trailer, but—"

He didn't wait. Dodging the man's grip, he raced up, threw the door open, and dived for the desk. The number of Mac's cell seemed endless, then there was a crackle of sound.

The policeman's bulk darkened the doorway. "You can't just—"

"*Shut up!*" Rob turned. "Mac? *Mac!*"

Noise.

People crying. His mother crying. A babble of voices, high and hysterical. Dan's voice and Rosa's. Nurses. Pandemonium.

"Mac! What's happening? What's happening?"

His godfather's voice was hoarse. "She's here, Rob. She's with us again."

"God." It was all he could say, could think. *"Oh God."*

"Talk to her," Mac growled.

The phone crackled. He heard breath and rustles. He heard the moving forest.

Then Chloe's whisper. "Rob?"

He gripped the phone so tight his hand throbbed. "Chloe," he breathed.

She sounded small. She sounded as if she wanted him.

"Where are you?" she sobbed. "You should be here."

He swallowed, made himself smile. "This is your time," he whispered. "Your time."

They all wanted to talk to him. He was to get a taxi and race there. His father whooped and gabbled nonsense; his mother could only sob. Finally Mac's voice came back, gruff and exhausted. "She'll sleep again for a few hours but get yourself here as soon as you can. She needs you, Rob." There was a pause. Then, "Where's Vetch?"

Rob scraped a hand down his face. He felt light-headed. "Home." Then he said, "Has she . . . is there anything around her neck?"

An empty second. Then, "No. Why?"

"I'll . . . explain. When I come."

Mac sounded sour and silly with joy. "I can't wait to hear that."

The phone clicked off.

On the steps of the trailer Rob stood and saw the sun through the trees. There were so few trees left.

Beyond them the downs stretched, green and smooth, small sheep on their back. The policeman scowled at him. "You'd better get home before I think better of it."

"I'm going, believe me."

He stumbled to the gate and looked back.

In its hollow, beyond the destroyed fence, Darkhenge stood silent and remote. But not still. It moved, and blurred, and at first Rob thought it was his eyes, tired and playing tricks on him, and then the movement became clear, and he understood that he was seeing the swarming of thousands of beetles, tiny wood-boring creatures, their hard carapaces glinting as they scrambled up from the soil.

The Unworld had sent its messengers to devour the henge.

By the time anyone realized, it would be eaten to the ground.

Rob smiled a weary smile. One day he'd do a painting of it. He would be the only one who ever could.

He'd leave it to Chloe to write the story.

AUTHOR'S NOTE

The story of Taliesin and Ceridwen will be found in Lady Guest's version of the Mabinogi. For more information and speculation on the poems, "The Battle of the Trees," the crane-skin bag, and the tree alphabet, I refer readers to Robert Graves's fascinating and complex book *The White Goddess: A Historical Grammar of Poetic Myth* (Faber, 1961) and John Matthews's intriguing *Taliesin: The Last Celtic Shaman* (Aquarian Press, 1991). My debt to both is obvious and freely acknowledged.